Keller's Fedora

Keller's
Fedora

LAWRENCE BLOCK

Subterranean Press 2017

First Edition

ISBN
978-1-59606-811-7

Subterranean Press
PO Box 190106
Burton, MI 48519

subterraneanpress.com

When the salesman asked him his hat size, Keller was stuck for an answer. Some years ago he'd come to New Orleans wearing a Homer Simpson baseball cap, which he'd managed to swap for a Saints cap. Remembering it now, it struck him as curious that a football team would embroider its logo on baseball caps, but he didn't think it was something he needed to dwell on.

His hat size? Aside from those two baseball caps, neither of which he'd actually picked out and purchased, he couldn't remember ever having had an actual hat. And baseball caps didn't come in sizes, did they? Weren't they all one-size-fits-all, with a little band with holes in it that you loosened or tightened accordingly?

"I'm not sure," he said.

The salesman, a plump fellow with a mustache trimmed to near-invisibility, cocked his head and narrowed his eyes. "I would say seven and three-eighths," he said, "and shall we see how close I am?"

He lifted a chocolate-brown fedora from its shelf and presented it to Keller, who placed it on his head. The salesman took hold of the brim, tilted it this way and that way, and stepped back, beaming. "Seven and three-eighths," he announced. "You could get away with seven and a quarter or seven and a half, but why make do when it's as easy to have a hat that fits you perfectly? Have a look."

Keller checked his reflection in the mirror, and there he was, same old Keller, except that he was wearing a hat.

"The classic fedora," the salesman said. "A true classic with a noble pedigree. The name comes from the title of a play that Victorien Sardou wrote for Sarah Bernhardt in 1882. The divine Sarah played the Princess Fedora and wore a hat quite like yours. And while I don't doubt she looked spectacular in it, I'd say you'd give her a run for her money. Not everyone can wear a fedora, you know."

"Oh?"

"It takes a certain *je ne sais quoi*," the man said. "A soupçon of *joie de vivre*. One must be at ease in a fedora, as you are so clearly at ease in yours."

Oh, brother, Keller thought. He said, "I was thinking gray."

"The brown does suit you, but let's have a look, shall we? Light gray or dark gray? But why not try them both?"

The shop, a haberdashery on Canal Street called Peller and Smythe, had both shades in Keller's size, and he tried them on in turn. "We also have black," the salesman said, "but if I may venture an opinion—"

"Not black," Keller said.

"Exactly. We're not really the black hat type, are we? And a good thing, I have to say."

"I think the dark gray," Keller said.

"And I'd say that's an excellent choice."

"MY GOODNESS," JULIA said.

"What do you think?"

"The man who went out for a loaf of bread," she said, "and came back with a hat."

"Was I supposed to buy bread?"

"No, it was just something to say. But you're full of surprises. I don't think I've ever seen you wearing a hat."

"No, probably not. When we're doing demolition on a job site, Donny and I have a couple of white painter's caps we'll put on. Or if we're painting something, for that matter. But nothing like this. It's a fedora."

"Well, I know that." She adjusted the brim. "You look like somebody I might see in a black-and-white movie on TCM."

"A private eye?"

"Or a gangster, but you couldn't look like a gangster."

"I couldn't?"

"No," she said. "You'd have to be the good guy."

⩘

IN THE MORNING he had breakfast with Jenny and walked her to school. "I'll be away for a while," he told her.

"To buy stamps," she said.

Most of his trips were to buy stamps, either for his own collection or, increasingly, for resale. This time he hadn't even packed a pair of tongs, let alone the Scott catalogue he used as a checklist.

"Well, to look at some stamps," he said. "I don't know if I'm actually going to buy any."

He decided on the way home that it bothered him to lie to his daughter, but he couldn't see a way around it. This would be the first solo trip in a long time that wasn't philatelic in nature, the first return in a couple of years to a profession he had to keep secret. Julia knew, of course. Julia had known all along, and had even played a role once.

But Jenny knew that he bought and sold stamps, and that he sometimes helped Uncle Donny fix up houses so that they could sell them. That was all she knew, and it would have been inappropriate, not to say upsetting and even dangerous, for her to know more.

Still, it bothered him.

∼∖⁄∼

HE'D PACKED THE night before, and by the time he got home Julia had already transferred his bag to the back seat of her Audi. He'd been bareheaded when he walked Jenny to school, but the fedora was on his head when he got into the passenger seat and buckled up.

"Ah," Julia said. "You bought it for your trip."

"I don't know why I bought it. I was planning on leaving it home."

"You've evidently changed your mind."

"I could still leave it in the car," he said.

But he didn't. She dropped him at the Amtrak station on Loyola, and he took off his hat to kiss her goodbye, and then put it back on again.

Inside, with his ticket already purchased in advance and two hours before his train was scheduled to depart, he bought a *Times-Picayune* and a cup of coffee and skimmed one while he sipped at the other. The coffee was all right—trust New Orleans to have acceptable coffee even in a train station—but the paper didn't hold his interest, and eventually he drifted back to the newsstand and browsed the rack of paperbacks.

Fully half the titles on display seemed to be by the same two writers, each of whom collaborated with a whole stable of co-writers.

Keller wondered what would happen if the two main guys should merge, through some sort of stock swap. They'd be a good bet to lock up every train and airport outlet in America, but could they get away with it? Would they run up against the Sherman Anti-Trust Act?

One book, by neither of the two, caught his eye, because for a half-second he thought it had his picture on the cover. Of course it wasn't his picture, the guy on the cover didn't look anything like Keller, but he was wearing Keller's hat, a dark gray fedora that looked exactly like the one on Keller's head.

Well, almost. The one on the cover had a bullet hole in the crown, with wisps of smoke suggesting it had been recently bestowed. If the near miss bothered the hat's wearer, you couldn't tell it by the expression of grim determination that he wore as easily as he wore the hat.

Call Him Jake was the book's title, and the publisher wanted you to know that it was the first volume in the Jake Dagger series. But it was the blurb that made Keller carry the book to the register and pay cash for it.

"*He's a private eye. His life is booze, babes, and bullets.*"

THE TRAIN WAS the City of New Orleans, and once in a while you still heard Arlo Guthrie's song about it. It left on time, a little before two, and was due in Chicago at nine the next morning. Keller had booked a roomette, and once he was settled in he took out his book and read a few pages.

Years ago, when he'd lived on the East Side of Manhattan a few blocks from the UN, a job had taken him clear across the country to Wyoming. He'd flown there and back, of course, and the state's population was lower for his having gone there, but what he remembered best was the book he bought before his flight.

Well, not the book. All he recalled of it was its blurb, and he remembered that much word for word: *"He rode a thousand miles to kill a man he'd never met."*

Hell of a line, he'd thought at the time. And he still thought so, but the one on *Call Him Jake* wasn't bad, either.

When you took a roomette, you were in the care of a porter, and Keller's introduced himself shortly after the train left the station. He said, "Mr. Edwards? My name is Ainslie, and I'll be with you all the way to Chicago," and went on to tell him about the diner and the café car, and that he'd make up the bed for him when he was ready to retire.

"So I don't forget you in the morning," Keller said, and palmed him a twenty. He'd taken enough trains in recent years to get in the habit of giving out his tips early on, so they could do him some good.

∽⁄⁄∼

KELLER SPENT SOME of his time with the book, but more of it looking out the window and letting his mind wander. He'd never minded flying, but what you had to go through at airports was a pain in the neck, and meant showing ID and turning up in no end of official records.

That didn't matter much if he was looking to make some widow an offer for her husband's stamp collection, but even then it was a nuisance. This trip, though, was a return to an earlier life, and he was literally riding a thousand miles (albeit more comfortably than if he were on horseback) to kill a man he'd never met—a man, in fact, whose name he didn't even know yet.

And learning that man's name, and other things about the fellow, would be the first order of business. He'd have to play private detective, and at this point the only thing he had going for him in that department was his hat.

And so, although there was nothing particularly gripping about *Call Him Jake*, he found himself dipping back into the book from time to time. Not for the promise of booze or babes or bullets, none of which held any real appeal for him. But on the chance that he might pick up some tradecraft.

SUNDAY HE'D TAKEN Jenny to the zoo in Audubon Park. "We can't see Spots," she said.

"No, we can't."

"Because Spots is dead," she said.

Spots had been the zoo's astonishingly rare white alligator, one of a clutch of seventeen blue-eyed hatchlings discovered in 1987. Spots had survived for twenty-eight years, which sounded like a long time for an alligator irrespective of its color, but Keller couldn't be sure of that. What he did know for certain was that Spots had died in September, and his passing had evidently impressed itself upon Jenny, because she'd taken note of it on every zoo visit since then.

"We had a wonderful time," he told Julia on their return. "Saw some old friends and met some new ones, including an Indonesian babirusa. It's like a wild pig-dog, with these tusks that curve up and back, and if it doesn't keep them filed down they'll grow into its skull and kill it."

"And not a moment too soon, I would think."

"Jenny thought it was terrific. She kept saying *babirusa* over and over, which is how I happen to remember its name."

"And Spots is still dead."

"I'm afraid so. I don't know that she's upset, but she's never failed to remark on it."

"Part of figuring out what death is, I guess."

"I guess. She wants to know if there's a stamp with a babirusa on it. I'll have to do some research."

"There must be," she said. "There's a stamp for everything, isn't there? Oh, before I forget. Dot called."

"Don't tell me she's in town."

"No, she called from Sedona. She was sorry to miss you, but even sorrier to miss a chance to talk to Jenny. There was something else she said."

"Oh?"

"She's been doing Pilates. And she was trying to find something to collect, but everything's too easy now that there's eBay. You don't get the thrill of the chase. But that's not what I'm supposed to tell you."

"Though it's true enough," he said, "but—"

"I remember. She said she'd been trying to reach your friend Pablo, and wondered if you knew how to get ahold of him. By the time I remembered who Pablo was, the conversation was over."

"Well," he said.

He went upstairs and found the Pablo phone in the back of his sock drawer. A while ago, he and Dot had each bought a burner phone, an unregistered prepaid device which they'd sworn to use only to call each other. Along the way she'd taken to calling him Pablo during conversations on that dedicated line, for no reason he could think of, and while that didn't last, the instrument itself would forever be the Pablo phone.

And, of course, it was every bit as dead as Spots the Alligator. He hooked it up to a charger, and after dinner he called the only number in its memory.

Halfway through the third ring, Dot picked up. "Ah," she said. "Pablo!"

"HERE'S THE THING," she said. "I know you're not doing work anymore, and I actually think that's great. You've got a wife and a kid, you've got the stamp business, and did Julia tell me you and your buddy are back in the business of flipping houses?"

"In a small way," he said. "The economy put us out of business, and then it turned around and let us back in."

"But between the stamps and the houses, and all that dough in the Caymans, you're in decent shape."

"That's right."

"That's what I thought, and I'm glad to hear it. I only called you because there's nobody else I can call, but so what? I'll tell him to find somebody else. I'm okay for dough myself, and just because I always want more doesn't mean I *need* more, you know?"

"Well."

"No reason to waste your time telling you about it. What's the point? Better for you to tell me something cute that Jenny said."

"Spots is dead."

"Well, I'm sorry to hear that, although I don't know that I'd call it cute. Poignant, maybe. Do I know who he is?"

"The white alligator."

"The white alligator. At the zoo?"

"Not anymore."

"No, I guess you can't keep the dead ones around. Look, I'll hang up, and you can put the Pablo phone away for another couple of years. I bet you had to charge it just now, didn't you?"

"It was dead."

"Same as mine. Dead as a white alligator, I'd have to say. So we can both forget what I called to tell you, and our next conversation can be on an open line."

Yes, I think that would be best. That was the sentence he heard in his mind. But what he said, to their mutual surprise, was, "Wait a minute."

IT WAS, AS she explained it, pretty straightforward. Until it wasn't.

"You've probably never heard of it," she said, "but there's a town in Illinois called Baker's Bluff."

"South and west of Chicago," he said.

"Don't tell me you've been there."

"I haven't."

"There's a stamp dealer there."

"Not that I know of."

"I give up."

"It was the birthplace of a man named Bronson Pettiford, who did something important in the early days of aviation. He was sometimes referred to as the third Wright Brother."

"Wilbur, Orville, and Bronson."

"Something like that," he allowed. "There was a stamp with his picture on it, standing next to an airplane no one in his right mind would set foot in, and they held the First Day ceremony at Baker's Bluff."

"An American stamp."

"Well, it would have to be, wouldn't it? The rest of the world never heard of Bronson Pettiford."

"As opposed to here in the good old U S of A, where the son of a bitch is a household word. But you don't collect American stamps, do you? I'll tell you, Keller, if I didn't know better it would make me doubt your patriotism, but I know you have your reasons."

"A person can't collect everything."

"See? There's a reason right there."

"And I may not collect US, but I read *Linn's* every week, and they report on new stamps and first day ceremonies, and this just happened to stick in my mind."

"But the point is you've never been there."

"Why would I go?"

"In a minute or two," she said, "you'll still be asking yourself the same question. Okay, there's a fellow in Baker's Bluff who's got a lot of money, which is always a desirable quality in a client. He's also got a beautiful trophy wife, and she's got a boyfriend. Does a subtle pattern begin to emerge?"

"It does have a familiar ring to it. I don't suppose he's got an iron-clad prenuptial agreement."

"He may," she said, "or he may not. But it doesn't matter, because he wants to keep her."

"He wants something to happen to the boyfriend."

"God, you're quick on the uptake. That's one thing I've always loved about you, Pablo."

He frowned. "You said this was something only I could handle," he said, "but it sounds pretty ordinary. Client has a wife, wife has a lover, client wants the lover out of the picture. I must be missing something. The last time there was a job that only I could be trusted with, the target was a young boy."

"And a stamp collector in the bargain, if I remember correctly."

"A very nice kid," Keller remembered. "First-rate collection of post-World War I German plebiscite issues. Allenstein."

"That was his name? Allen Stein?"

"It was one of the plebiscite regions. In 1920, the citizens of Allenstein voted overwhelmingly to remain part of Germany. Anyway, I got a card from him at Christmas."

"Did it have a nice stamp on it? Never mind, you don't have to answer that. I don't know how kinky the trophy wife may be, but I think we can take it as a given that her boyfriend's over eighteen."

"Then what's the problem? You've got other people you could call."

"Two or three," she said, "and I'm not crazy about any of them, but when something's simple and straightforward I can work with them."

"But taking out a boyfriend in Illinois is too much for them? What am I missing here?"

"Nothing that I'm not missing myself, Pablo."

He was forming a question when she dropped the rest of the shoe.

"The son of a bitch knows she's got a lover," she said. "What he doesn't know is who it is."

※

"SO THERE YOU go," she said. "I know what you're thinking, and it's something he thought of himself. What he needs is a private detective. But fortunately he stopped right there."

"Fortunately?"

"If he hires a private eye, and if the private eye brings him a name and a photograph, and if a week or two later the guy in the photograph turns up dead, then what happens?"

"Oh, right."

"The private eye's a problem," she said, "because if he was bright enough to find the boyfriend in the first place, he's certainly bright enough to figure out what happened to him. And either he turns up with his hand out or he goes straight to the cops but either way it's bad news for the client."

He saw where this was going.

"So it has to be the same person for both parts of the job," he said.

"There you go."

"First to identify the boyfriend, and then to do something about him."

"Something permanent."

"Dot, I'm not a private detective."

"Who said you were? Pablo, you're a stamp guy and a construction guy. When you pick up a magnifying glass, it's not to look for clues. It's to check perficulations."

"Perforations," he said. "And for that you use a perforation gauge."

"My life is richer for knowing that. But think back to Buffalo, will you? That kid you saved?"

"I don't know that I saved him. I didn't kill him. That's not the same thing as saving him."

"What happened to his uncle?"

"No more than he deserved."

"The uncle was our client," she reminded him. "But we didn't know that. He worked through a cutout, so all you knew was that there were at least three people who had a reason to want the boy dead. And you investigated, the same way a private detective would do."

"I just poked around a little. Kept my eyes and ears open, talked to people, worked it out."

"Right."

"You think I could do this," he said. "Go to Baker's Bluff, play Sherlock Holmes—"

"More like Sam Spade, I'd think. Or Philip Marlowe. When they make the movie, Humphrey Bogart can play you."

"Isn't it a little late for that?"

"They'll make an old movie," she said. "Black and white, with men in hats. And I don't know if you could do it, Pablo, or why you'd even consider it, to tell you the truth. All I know is I don't know anybody else I'd even suggest it to, and there was a time when I'd have handed it to you right away, and you'd have been on it like a mongoose on a cobra. But you're pretty much retired, and I'd be retired if I weren't such a greedy old lady, and you've got stamps and houses to keep you busy, so tell me to forget it and I'll let my phone go dead again."

Baker's Bluff, Illinois. How would he even get there?

"Pablo? Don't tell me you hung up."

"No, I'm here," he said. "Look, don't put the phone away, all right? Give me an hour and I'll call you back."

∽⁄⁄∼

"IT'S CRAZY," HE told Julia. "In the first place I've got other things to do. And it's not as though we needed the money."

"That's true."

"And it's complicated. First I'd have to figure out who the target should be, before I even do anything."

"That doesn't make it simple."

"And he could be an easy target or a hard one," he said. "There's no way to know."

"You want another cup of coffee?"

"Sure, but sit there, I'll get it. Another thing, I might have to have contact with the client. I'd try to run everything through Dot, because it's never a good idea for the client to be able to identify you. The cops pick him up, he falls apart under questioning, and there you are."

"But if all the contact is through Dot—"

"That's better. And if I absolutely had to talk to him, it'd be on a burner."

"The Pablo phone."

"No, but one like it. Buy it, talk to him, toss it in the river. If there's a river near Baker's Bluff."

"I suppose a lake would do in a pinch."

"Or a storm drain. Donny could get along without me for a week or two. There's stuff that needs doing, but I don't have to be

| 20 |

there when it gets done. And all I have to do is mention the stamp business, and that's as much of a reason for my absence as he'd need."

"Well, that's good."

"I'd miss you and Jenny."

"And we'd miss you. But it's the same when you go on a buying trip. You're away for a few days, and then you come back, and we're happy to see you."

"I suppose an occasional break is good."

"They say it makes the heart grow fonder," she said, "although I can't imagine being any fonder of you than I already am. You know, it comes down to one thing, really. Do you want to go? And the answer seems to be that you do."

"Why? It's not as though I enjoy killing. As soon as it's done, I do everything I can to put it out of my mind."

"Erasing the memory."

"As well as I can. But—"

"You want to do it," she said, "because it's who you are."

"A man who kills people."

"Except that's not the point of it. It's the resolution, but the point is solving a particular kind of a problem."

"I guess. I wonder."

"You wonder what?"

"Well, when Dot told me the complication—"

"Not knowing the identity of the target."

"Right. That would have been the time for me to tell her to forget it."

"But it's when you found yourself getting drawn in."

"That's right. 'Oh, that's really crazy and stupid,' I said to myself."

"'So sign me up!'"

"Just about. That's insane, isn't it? Perverse, anyway."

"It makes it more interesting," she said. "You like things to be interesting."

☀

THE TRAIN HAD just pulled out of Greenwood, Mississippi, when he went to the dining car. It was still light out, and while he'd brought his book with him, he spent most of his time looking out the window, wondering who lived out there and what their lives were like. And maybe someone out there was looking at the passing train, and wondering about the people on it.

His meal was a leisurely one, and it was dark by the time he returned to his roomette. He read for an hour or so, then got Ainslie to turn the facing seats into a bed. He undressed and killed the lights and got under the blanket, and lay there wondering how much sleep he was likely to get.

Next thing he knew they were coming into Kankakee. That was in the song, wasn't it? He looked at his watch, and it was a quarter after seven, and time for breakfast. And when he got back from breakfast, Ainslie had restored the roomette's original configuration, and his dark gray fedora was perched on the opposite seat, along with his suitcase.

He could have checked the suitcase. You could do that before your train was available for boarding, and pick it up at Baggage Claim when you arrived. He hadn't, figuring there might be something in it that he wanted en route, and of course there wasn't.

He was wearing the hat when they got to Chicago, and he'd have been carrying the suitcase if Ainslie hadn't insisted on performing that task for him. Once Keller was on the platform, Ainslie handed over the suitcase. "Here you go, Mr. Edwards," he said. "Now you have a fine stay in Chicago, hear?"

A brief one, Keller thought.

He walked through the train station, found the queue of taxis, and took one to O'Hare Airport. Half an hour later, when he emerged from the taxi, he stopped being Nicholas Edwards.

~\|/~

THAT WAS THE name on his Louisiana driver's license and his US passport, the name by which everybody in both New Orleans and the philatelic world knew him. His wife's name was Julia Roussard Edwards, and his daughter's name was Jenny Edwards. The Edwards name had come from a gravestone, and in the aftermath of Hurricane Katrina it had been easy enough to explain away lost records and get a copy of a dead infant's birth certificate as his own. Everything else had followed in due course, and at this point it would be a neat trick for anyone to prove that he was not Nicholas Edwards.

Which was just as well. There was still an open file somewhere, with one John Paul Keller of New York, NY, being sought in connection with a high-profile homicide in Des Moines, Iowa. Nobody was pressing the case, and it seemed likely they thought he was dead if they thought about him at all, but it was reason enough to protect his new identity.

And one way to protect it was to put it in mothballs for the time being.

~\|/~

IN THE PASSENGER terminal, he looked for the Hertz counter, then walked on past it to the men's room. There he switched his wallet for another, slimmer one. Nicholas Edwards now reposed in a zippered compartment in his suitcase, and the wallet on his hip identified him as James J. Miller, of Waco, Texas. There was a Texas driver's license in that name, a pair of valid credit cards, and the usual filler—membership cards in hotel loyalty programs and the American Automobile Association, a courtesy card from the Ft. Worth Chamber of Commerce, and last year's calendar, the gift of an insurance agent in Galveston.

All he had to show was the driver's license and James Miller's Visa card. They had his reservation, gave him a Japanese compact with the tank filled, and told him he could bring it back empty.

"But we had a gentleman two weeks ago who cut it a little too close," the attendant told him. She was not quite flirty, but almost. "He made it into the lot, and he got halfway up the aisle, and the engine went dry and cut out. Now you just might want to give yourself a little more leeway."

Touched his wrist as she spoke the last line. Well, semi-flirty, anyway.

"I'll be careful," he assured her, and gave her a smile, and went off to collect his car.

JAMES J. MILLER had booked a ground-floor room at the Super Eight motel on the north edge of Baker's Bluff, and by one o'clock Keller was checked in and as unpacked as he felt the need to be. He'd brought three phones, and they were lined up on the coffee table, looking virtually identical.

Well, not entirely so. One was an iPhone, and it was the phone he carried all the time, except when he forgot and left it on the bedside table. He'd used it once since he left New Orleans, calling Julia as the train was approaching Chicago, telling her where he was and that all was well. Then he'd turned it off, and could only hope that would keep it from pinging off the nearest tower, telling the world where he was. It couldn't ping if it was turned off, could it?

Hell, how was he supposed to know what it could or couldn't do? Maybe he should have left it home.

He put it away for now and considered the other two phones, turning them over, studying them. It wasn't really all that hard to tell them apart, not if you really looked at them. The Pablo phone was older by several years, and looked it, with scratches on the case.

He turned it on and placed a call. It rang a couple of times, and then Dot picked up.

"Well, I'm here," he said. "Now what?"

∼⁄⁄⁄∼

WHEN HE WAS done talking, he put on his jacket, straightened his tie. The fedora was on the bed, and wasn't that supposed to be bad luck? Not a fedora specifically, but any hat on a bed? It seemed to him that he'd read something to that effect, and thought it might be a superstition in the world of the theater, like telling one's friends to break a leg rather than wishing them good luck. And never saying the word *Macbeth*, but referring to it as *The Scottish Play*.

There were explanations for these superstitions, and he could find out what they were and where they came from by calling up Google on his iPhone, but then it would be pinging off towers, so the hell with it.

Still, he picked up the hat and looked for a place to put it. The closet shelf? No, that would put it out of sight and thus out of mind, and all too easily left behind.

He'd worn it when he checked in, and it seemed to him that the desk clerk was more solicitous and respectful than usual. He'd put it down to Midwestern courtesy, but now he wondered if the hat might have had something to do with it.

It was on his head when he left the room.

∼⁄⁄⁄∼

FROM DOT HE'D learned that the client's name was Todd Overmont. He commuted every day to his office in Chicago, where he did something with commodities. Something profitable, Keller decided, once the Hertz car's GPS had led him to Overmont's house, a massive affair on Robin's Nest Drive that might have been inspired by Mount Vernon.

Keller parked on the other side of the street, where he could keep an eye on the house and monitor activity coming or going. This was one of the things detectives did, he reminded himself. They called it being on a stakeout, and according to Jake Dagger, the hardest part was coping with boredom.

After half an hour during which there'd been no activity to monitor, coming or going, he could see the truth in Jake Dagger's observation. Another identical half hour confirmed it, but by then he'd come to realize that coping with boredom was the second hardest part of a stakeout.

Needing to pee was worse.

He found a gas station, topped up the Subaru's tank, bought a wide-mouthed glass jar of a fruit-flavored iced tea, and visited the restroom. After he'd done what he'd come there to do, he uncapped the iced tea, poured it down the sink, and returned to the car carrying the empty jar, ready to cope with problems that apparently never troubled Jake "Iron Bladder" Dagger.

He didn't need the GPS to get him back to the Overmont house. He found it on his own, and as he made the turn onto Robin's Nest Drive, he saw a car heading off to the west. That was nothing remarkable, cars did that sort of thing, although there'd been precious little traffic on Robin's Nest Drive during the hour he'd spent staked out there. But out of the corner of his eye he caught the Overmont garage door descending the final couple of feet, and put two and two together.

There was, he realized, a little more to this stakeout business than he'd thought.

Up ahead, the car he'd seen was making a right turn. Keller clapped his fedora on his head and leaned on the gas pedal.

ONCE HE'D CAUGHT up with her, following Melania Overmont turned out to be surprisingly easy. She was driving a big silver Lexus, not a hard car to distinguish from its fellows, and if she took her marriage vows as seriously as she took the Baker's Bluff traffic regulations, then the client had nothing to worry about. She kept the Lexus well under the posted speed limit, came to a full stop at stop signs, and did all this without giving any indication that she'd noticed a white Subaru in her rearview mirror.

Piece of cake, Keller thought.

If it was Melania Overmont. He got close enough to determine that the driver was a woman with shoulder-length blonde hair, but Dot hadn't provided a description, and for all he knew he might be following a cleaning woman, dispatched on an errand for her employer.

That seemed a little more likely when the Lexus braked at the entrance to a strip mall, waited courteously for an oncoming car to pass, and then turned left into the mall, pulling into a space in front of Pioneer Super Food Mart. Keller waited for a break in traffic, then followed her in and eased the Subaru into a space three slots to the left of the Lexus.

He killed the engine and waited for her to get out of the car. Instead she backed out of her spot.

He'd been made, he thought. She'd pulled in just to see if he'd follow her, and when he did she'd identified him, and now she'd shake him the way nobody shook Jake Dagger, and—

Instead, she maneuvered the car to and fro, and tucked it into the parking space immediately next to his.

Huh?

Why on earth would she do that? Because she'd spotted him? No, that didn't make any sense at all. She'd parked her car in a perfectly good space, and now she'd forsaken it for this space, the only distinguishing characteristic of which was that it was right next to Keller's Subaru. What could she possibly—

Oh.

The first space, he saw, was reserved for handicapped parking. You could get a ticket if you parked there without the requisite sticker.

If Keller had brought a newspaper along he'd pretend to read it, but he didn't have anything, not even the Jake Dagger book. He sat very still and watched out of the corner of his eye as she got out of the Lexus. She never looked in his direction, and once she'd closed her door and headed for the market entrance he gave her his full attention.

Well, she wasn't a cleaning woman, unless she'd somehow reported to work in tight white jeans and a scoop-necked blue blouse, with rings on her fingers and, for all he knew, bells on her toes. She was a good-looking woman, no question, and you could see why Todd Overmont might think she was cheating on him, because there was something about her that suggested she'd be capable of it.

Nothing he could define, really. Nothing he could put his finger on...

He sat behind the wheel, took his hat off, put his hat back on again. Should he enter the market and confirm that she was there? It's not as though he'll be expected to file a report: *2:38 pm. Subject entered Pioneer Super Food Mart. 2:41 pm. Subject took two boxes of breakfast cereal from shelf, compared ingredients, put one box back and added other to cart. 2:45 pm. Subject opened egg carton to make sure all of its contents were unbroken...*

He stayed where he was, wondering why it was taking so long, and found out when she finally emerged, trailing a gawky teenager who was pushing a cart. He followed her to the car, and Keller watched as she opened the lid of the trunk and stood aside to let the boy stow bag after bag of groceries in it.

Couldn't be more innocent, he thought. Woman's a housewife doing what housewives do.

And now the last bag was in the trunk, and the lid closed, and Mrs. Overmont was reaching into her purse. She drew out a dollar, hesitated for a moment, then added another dollar.

Was that a generous tip? A skimpy one? Keller, who carried his own groceries whenever he did the shopping, had no real frame of reference. The kid hadn't had to carry anything, all he'd done was push a cart twenty or thirty yards from the door to where she'd parked her car. Moving her groceries a bag at a time from the cart to the trunk was hardly heavy labor, and the total time involved was what, five minutes? It seemed to Keller that a single dollar would have been plenty, but then you had to weigh in the fact that she was a rich woman driving an expensive car, and maybe that was enough to bump the tip to the two-dollar level.

As if it mattered. Keller shook his head, marveling at his own propensity to overthink everything, and then Melania Overmont did something unusual. She looked around, to the left and to the right, as if to assure herself that she was not being observed.

If she'd turned all the way around she'd have seen Keller. But she didn't, and he went on watching her, because that little move of hers was definitively furtive, and he had to wonder why. All she was doing was tipping the kid, and what did she care who saw her give him a couple of bucks?

And he watched, playing close attention, as she held out the two dollars in her left hand. The boy held out a hand to take the money, and Melania extended her other hand, her right hand, and reached for the boy's crotch.

Keller stared.

And went on staring, because this wasn't going to be a quick grope and goodbye. She'd stepped closer to the kid, so that he couldn't see what she was doing with her hand, but it didn't take a genius to figure it out. All he had to do was watch the boy's face, as it ran the gamut of emotions from surprise to shock to excitement to what could only be satisfaction.

"A HAND JOB, Pablo?"

"I guess that's the term."

"In a strip mall? In front of a supermarket? In the middle of Illinois?"

"And then she put the two dollars in his hand," he said, "and closed his fingers around it. And kissed her own fingers, and patted him on the check."

"And got in her car and drove away. I trust you followed her."

"Straight back to her house. She had to put away her groceries."

"And wash her hands," Dot said. "And she's there now?"

"She'd have to be. She hasn't gone anywhere. She left the garage door up while she dealt with her bags of groceries, but it's down now, and as far as I can tell she's still in the house."

"And you're parked across the street. Well, I guess the thing to do is sit tight."

"For as long as it takes," he said. "I've got the jar, so I'll be fine."

"I have no idea what that means."

"It's not important. Dot, am I supposed to do anything about the kid?"

"The kid? What kid? Oh, you mean the grocery boy?"

"Right. I mean, he's a big kid, he's got to be eighteen or nineteen."

"He could be a college graduate," she said. "An English major, working away at the only job he could get."

"That'd make him what, twenty-one? Twenty-two?"

"More, if he went to grad school."

"I don't think—"

"Pablo, what difference does it make?"

"Just that it's not Buffalo all over again."

"He's not a little kid with a stamp collection."

"No."

"In other words, he's old enough to stop getting older."

"From an ethical standpoint," he said, "I don't see it as a problem. But is this what the client wants?"

"Pablo, do you figure the Hand Job Kid is her steady squeeze?"

"Well—"

"So to speak. You did say he looked surprised, didn't you?"

"Astonished. She was driving away and he was standing there with his mouth hanging open, like he couldn't believe what just happened to him."

"I'd say he gets to live another day, Pablo."

"That's what I thought, but—"

"But the possibility had to be raised. I agree with you there. But this was just her way of saying thank you. 'Here's two bucks and a hand job, young man, because I'm not the type to blow you off with a mere dollar.'"

"So to speak," he said.

"Fair enough. She's a piece of work, our Mrs. Overmont. I can't wait to see what she comes up with next."

"Oh," he said.

"You say something, Pablo?"

"The garage door's going up," he reported.

"In a minute she'll be on her way."

"I don't see her. Oh, there she is, at the front door. She's standing on the stoop."

"Clutching a small bottle of hand lotion."

"No," he said.

"On her way to the car."

"I don't think so, because she's not carrying her purse. Would she go out without it? Oh."

"Oh?"

"A white car turning into the driveway," he said. "Except it's more of a van. There's a man driving, has a sort of Marlboro Man look to him."

"That's going back a ways, the Marlboro Man. Didn't they all die of lung cancer?"

"She's waving. I think she's glad to see him."

"You don't figure that's a gun in her pocket?"

"And now she's back inside the house. She just closed the door."

"You know, this is wonderful, Pablo. Getting a play-by-play like this, it's almost like I'm watching it with my own two eyes. Why'd you stop?"

"Because nothing's happening," he said. "Oh, there you go."

"What?"

"The garage door's closing. I guess she walked over and pressed the button. The garage is attached, he can go in straight from there, the way she did with the groceries."

"So it's closed and his van's in there."

"Right."

"He could be the gardener," she said, "or the electrician, or the guy who takes care of the pool. The pool guy, I guess you call him."

"Is there a pool?"

"How would I know? You're the one who's sitting there. If you can't see whether or not there's a pool in the backyard—"

"If there is, I couldn't see it from here. The house is in the way."

"My guess," she said, "is it's probably not the pool guy. Or the cable guy, or the guy to fix the furnace or change the filters on the air-conditioners. What do you figure, central air or window units?"

"Huh?"

"Never mind, because if it was any of those guys his car would be parked in plain sight in the driveway, not stashed away in the garage next to her Mercedes."

"Lexus."

"Whatever. I think you're done with the detecting part, Pablo. Now it's time to switch hats."

"What did you just say?"

"That you can quit being Sherlock Holmes and do what you were born to do."

"You said something about hats."

"It's an expression, for God's sake. Switching hats, meaning playing a different role."

He took the fedora from his head, looked at it, put it back on again. "Never mind," he said. "I was confused for a minute there." Something occurred to him. "Dot, do I need to get into the house and take pictures?"

"What, of the two of them in a compromising position?"

"Well, do I?"

There was a pause, and he wondered if perhaps the Pablo phone had gone dead. Then she said, "Maybe I didn't make this clear. He's not looking to divorce the woman."

"I know that, but—"

"In fact he's very clear that he doesn't want anything to happen to her."

"I got that, but—"

"All the man wants," she said, "is for the other man in her life to stop being in her life. Or in anybody's life, including his own."

"I just thought he might want proof," he said, "that we didn't, you know, just pick somebody at random."

She thought it over. She said, "Okay, our client doesn't know who the guy is, so how does he know we've picked the right man. Is that what you mean?"

"I couldn't have put it better myself."

"So it would appear. And you have a point."

There was a pause, but this time he knew the line was intact. He could tell she was thinking.

She said, "Okay, he's gonna have to take our word for it. The thing is, you have to be positive. Because if the Marlboro Man turns out to be her brother Charlie, or some butch queen who dropped in to give her some advice on where to put the sofa—"

"That wouldn't be good."

"So check him out," she said. "You don't need evidence to show the client, just so long as you're convinced. After that, you know what you have to do."

"Right."

"And you're okay? Because it might be a while before he's done in there."

His hand reached for the empty iced tea jar. "No problem," he said. "I'm set."

☀

KELLER HAPPENED TO be looking at the garage door when it began its ascent. By then it was getting on for five in the afternoon, and he'd found himself thinking about the empty jar. It was a comfort to have it there, but the actual business of peeing in it was something he thought he'd put off as long as he could. He already felt conspicuous, sitting in a parked car on a street where few cars were parked. It helped that there was very little traffic, and no pedestrian traffic except for two boys, one of them dribbling a basketball, the other making a half-hearted attempt to get it away from him. They dribbled off down the street and turned at the corner, and neither of them gave Keller any notice.

Still, there he was, with his license plate visible to any citizen who cared to make a note of it. Part of the time he wore the hat and part of the time he didn't, but what difference did that make? It was off his head and on the seat beside him when the Overmont garage door went up, and that got his full attention. He waited for a glimpse of either or both of them, wishing they'd walk out arm in arm, pausing for a warm embrace and a quick grope before the guy got behind the wheel.

But if that happened he never saw it, because all he could see from where he sat was the rear end of the white van, and it was too deep in the shadows for him to make out a license plate. Then the engine started up and the van backed out of the garage.

By the time Keller got his engine started, the van had pulled out into the street, then turned and headed off in a direction opposite to the one Keller was facing. He had to turn around, and his quarry was already vanishing from sight, taking a left two blocks away.

Keller set off after him.

WHATEVER MELANIA OVERMONT and her presumed lover had in common, it wasn't a shared attitude toward traffic laws. She'd been a cinch to follow, always under the speed limit, pausing to give other drivers the right of way, and acting at all times like a teenager determined to pass a driving test.

Mr. Marlboro, on the other hand, was given to quick starts, sudden bursts of acceleration, abrupt left turns that forced oncoming drivers to hit the brakes, and showed a tendency to regard the speed limit as a minimum.

On the highway, it was hard to keep up with the van. On Harding Boulevard, in rush-hour traffic, how were you supposed to distinguish one white van from all the others? A couple of times he thought he'd lost the trail, but then he'd pick it up again. After forty-five minutes of this, the white van sailed through an intersection even as the light was turning from amber to red. Keller, three cars back, didn't even have a chance to run the red light, but did what he could to keep his man in sight.

Was that him? Was he making a right turn?

The light turned, finally, and the car immediately in front of Keller moved forward, finally, and Keller set off in search of the white van. A quarter of a mile along he turned where he thought the van might have turned, and found it parked in front of an establishment that sold wholesale and retail plumbing supplies.

Which figured, because the van had the name and address of that very firm lettered on its side panels. And that set it apart from the unmarked white van Keller had been following.

Jesus, had he lost the son of a bitch? He'd had the sense to memorize the license plate, and that'd be great if he had Jake Dagger's ring of friends on and off the police force. ("I used to be a cop, but when you carry a badge you've got to do things by the book. And sometimes a man just has to throw the book away.") Or the kind of charm that would win him a favor from a chirpy girl at the local Bureau of Motor Vehicles. ("I'm not supposed to do this, Jake. But shucks, just this once…") Right. But Keller wouldn't know whom to call, or what to say if he reached the appropriate person.

Hell.

He'd never really noticed how many white vans there were. And you couldn't quit on a parking lot just because you found a van that turned out to be the wrong one, because there might well be another white van in the next aisle or the one after that, and it could be the right one.

Or it could be another wrong one.

Finally, at the back of a freestanding frame building that could have used a coat of paint, he found three white vans parked side by side. And the one in the middle, by God, was the Marlboro Man's.

Keller, parking his car, realized just how long it had been since that gas station rest room. He glanced at the iced tea jar, glanced at the fedora, and left them both where they were.

He got out of the car, and just as he was closing the door he changed his mind, reached for the fedora, placed it on his head and adjusted the brim.

But never mind the jar. There'd be a men's room. Any place called the Wet Spot, any place with a jukebox that loud, really had to have a men's room.

⎯⎯⎯⎯⎯⎯

THE MARLBORO MAN was standing at the bar, hoisting a beer with a couple of buddies. Keller saw him when he walked in, went straight to the men's room, then spotted the guy again a few minutes later—still at the bar, still on his feet, still holding what might have been the same beer, which he was drinking straight from its long-necked bottle.

There was an unoccupied stool at the bar, and Keller took it. To his left were two men wearing White Sox caps, and to his right, on the other side of a second unoccupied stool, was a man with a plaid shirt and a cowboy hat.

Keller felt vindicated. He was right to have worn the fedora. Around here an uncovered head would stick out like a sore thumb.

The man in the cowboy hat was one of the Marlboro Man's two buddies, and looked enough like him to be, well, a stunt double, say. In fact they both looked like Hollywood stunt men, or what he assumed Hollywood stunt men would look like. Big men, rangy men, physical men.

Buddy Number Two was smaller, but wiry. He was wearing a railroad cap, striped blue denim with a short bill. Keller wasn't sure why they called it that, he took a lot of trains himself and had never seen a railroad employee wearing one, but maybe you were more apt to encounter them on freight trains. Maybe engineers wore them.

The cap's wearer could have been a stunt double himself, Keller decided, but for a smaller hero. Tom Cruise's stunt double, say.

Keller ordered a beer, took a preliminary sip from it when it came. The bartender was a woman with too many tattoos, and Keller realized she was the only woman in the place.

Jesus, was it a gay bar? It had the kind of aggressively masculine vibe you ran across in places with names like Rawhide and Boots & Saddle. This one was called the Wet Spot, but that could be some kind of gay double entendre, couldn't it?

Was any of that possible? Was the Marlboro Man Melania's interior decorator after all?

"Man, you're too much. Has she got a sister? That's what I want to know."

That was the man on Keller's right, the cowboy hat. The Marlboro Man replied that, if she had a sister, well, don't get any ideas, good buddy, because all that would mean was a three-way.

"Oh, man," said Tom Cruise's stunt double. "Oh man, oh man, oh man."

Cowboy Hat: "Like she'd be up for it."

Marlboro Man: "Melania? Haven't found anything yet she's not up for."

Tom Cruise (sounding a little drunk): "But with her own sister?"

Marlboro Man: "Dude, she hasn't got a sister."

Cowboy Hat: "Thing about a three-way, it's never everything you want it to be."

Tom Cruise: "If she hasn't got a sister—"

Marlboro Man: "You saying there's something wrong with a three-way?"

Tom Cruise: "—how are you gonna fuck her?"

Cowboy Hat: "Just that it's not as good as you hope."

Marlboro Man: "Well, shit, what is?"

Tom Cruise: "What I wanna know—"

Marlboro Man: "Dude, shut up. What I am is lucky she hasn't got a sister, or anybody else who wants to play, because that woman wears me out all by her lonesome."

Tom Cruise: "All I'm trying to say—"

But Keller didn't wait to find out what he was trying to say. He'd heard enough.

⚹

THREE WHITE VANS, side by side by side, and it was a good thing he'd taken note of the license number. Still, he could have ruled out the one on the right, which bore a generic company name ("R & D Assoc.") along with a phone number. And the one on the left, unmarked by paint, had a damaged rear bumper and a broken taillight.

The one in the middle, the Marlboro Man's van, had its doors locked. That figured, and Keller had tried the doors with no real hope they'd be open. You went through the motions, that's all, and he stepped to the rear of the van and went through them again with the hatch at the back, and what do you know?

Open.

First, Keller went to his Subaru, unlocked it, transferred the fedora from his head to the seat. He felt a little silly doing so, he was wasting valuable time, but he didn't want anything to happen to the hat—or, worse by far, for it to be left behind. He thought about putting it on the floor, where it would be out of sight and no temptation to passing thieves, and then decided he was being ridiculous.

He locked the car and went back to the three vans, and the middle van's hatch was still unlocked. He raised it and climbed in, clambering over all the gear you'd expect to find in the back of the guy's van—golf clubs, fishing tackle, a tool box, an array of unboxed tools, an old denim jacket, a tire iron, a hammer, a set of Allen wrenches—

There were almost too many options.

And way too much time to weigh them. Keller picked up the hammer and hunkered down on the left, right behind where the driver would sit. This wasn't the first time he'd waited in an unoccupied vehicle, and on one previous occasion he'd had an improvised garrote. Which, now that he thought about it, was really the only kind there was, because you couldn't go into a store and buy a ready-made garrote.

Though he supposed that could change overnight. All you needed was a powerful lobby, a group calling itself the National Garrote Association, say, and funded by an international cartel of garrote manufacturers, fully prepared to throw a lot of money at legislators while citing the relevant constitutional amendment. Probably not the one guaranteeing freedom of speech, because speech was difficult with a wire around your throat, and anyway nobody had the right to cry "Garrote!" in a crowded vehicle, and—

He never expected to drift off, not in such an uncomfortable position, but his thoughts drifted and his mind ambled along after them, and if he wasn't technically asleep, he was anything but bright-eyed and alert.

Until the argument woke him.

His immediate reaction to the three voices, three vaguely familiar voices at that, was an attempt to incorporate them into his dream. Then one of them said, "He can't drive, the sonofabitch is shitfaced," and another said, "Who you callin' a sonofabitch, you sonofabitch?" and he came fully awake while Cowboy Hat and Marlboro Man argued over who would give Tom Cruise a ride home.

It was like a custody battle over an unwanted child. "You take him!" "Hell no, *you* take him!" The child, meanwhile, insisted he'd be just fine on his own, and Keller got the feeling they'd had this argument before. It ended with Tom Cruise's stunt double, insisting on his statutory right to drive drunk or sober, getting into his van and pulling out. Keller braced himself, expecting to hear brakes squeal or worse, but heard neither.

That left two of them, Cowboy Hat and Marlboro Man, and if they weren't as drunk as their friend, neither were they sober. And so they stood between the two remaining vans having the sort of conversation one might expect them to have, and Keller's heart sank when Cowboy Hat said, "You know what? He's the one who was drunk, am I right or am I right?"

"One or the other," Marlboro Man agreed.

"And he went home, so how about you and I kick back one more beer before we go?"

"What, back in there? Back in the Wet Spot?"

"Why not?"

"Too many tattoos."

"What, the gal behind the bar? Ol' Maggie?"

"Way too many tattoos."

"Yeah, like you wouldn't do her if you had the chance."

"Did her once."

"Bullshit."

"She was drunk, I was drunk, all I remember is we did it. Woke up to a room full of tattoos. Whole lot you don't get to see when she's got her clothes on."

"You don't want to go back for one more beer? On account of tattoos?"

God, this was endless. Was there a way to get out of the car and take them both out? There wasn't, of course, not without a gun on full auto, and all he had was a hammer.

"Got it," Cowboy Hat said. "The Spotted Tiger."

"On Quincy? Love that place."

"So I'll meet you there. Or you want to ride with me?" Keller held his breath. "No, we should take both vans, in case you want to go home before I do."

Keller released his breath.

"Me? You'll be the one wants to leave first."

"Me? Hell, man, you're the pussy."

"Always bringin' up pussy, man. You want to smell my finger?"

And a little more banter, and Keller thought he was going to lose his mind, and then the doors of two vans were opening, the one he was in and the one on the right, and Keller's grip tightened on the hammer, because right now was the tricky part. If Marlboro Man happened to look in back while he was getting behind the wheel—

But he didn't. He settled himself in the driver's seat, slid the door shut, got his key in the ignition on the first try. On the right, Cowboy Hat was doing the same, and his engine started first. He gunned it, and now Marlboro Man answered in kind, and the two idiots took turns revving their engines, neither of them putting his van in gear, neither of them going anywhere.

Fifty-fifty, Keller thought. If Cowboy Hat drove away first, he'd swing the hammer and end it. If Marlboro Man led the way, he'd have to wait it out, see what opportunity presented itself along the way or at the Spotted Tiger.

Oh, the hell with it.

"YOU JUST WENT ahead," Dot said. "Pablo, I don't know how you found the nerve."

"I was trying to think it through," he said, "and it seemed to me that what I was doing was overthinking it."

"Oh? Whatever gave you that idea?"

He was in his room at the Super 8. The first thing he'd done, after using the room phone to call Amtrak's 800 number, was get out of his clothes and under the shower. He was wearing fresh clothes now, and seated in the unit's comfortable chair. And on the Pablo phone, talking to Dot.

"I couldn't wait," he said. "Sooner or later he'd have to sense my presence and turn around, you know? So I hauled off and swatted him on the temple."

"And the cowboy just drove off into the sunset?"

"Sunset was a couple of hours ago," he said. "But that's pretty much what happened. First thing he did was gun his engine, and then when my guy didn't respond—"

"Which he couldn't, with his skull caved in."

"—he went and gunned it again, and then I guess he figured the game was over."

"I'll say."

"I was waiting for him to come see what was wrong. He was on the right, so all he had to do was look in through the window on the passenger side, or the windshield in front. And he'd see the guy and figure he passed out or had a stroke or something, and he'd come around the van and try to help him, and I'd have a shot at him."

"With your hammer. What's the saying?"

"What saying?"

"'When your only tool is a hammer, every problem looks like a nail.' But you didn't have to nail him, did you?"

"No," he said. "He never got out of his van. He gunned the engine one last time and then backed up and drove away."

"And your Marlboro Man was dead as a doornail."

Well, was he? He was certainly out cold, but Keller hadn't bothered to take his pulse. Simpler to swing the hammer a second time, with a blow that left nothing to chance.

"The job's done," he assured her.

He waited while she switched phones and called the client. "I didn't tell him much," she reported. "Just that his problem's been solved, and where to send the money. I didn't have a name to give him, because you never told me."

"I never knew it myself."

"You found him," she said, "without knowing who you found. Well, that's a first. I'll tell you, the client couldn't believe it happened so fast, and do you want to know something, Pablo? I'm pretty impressed myself."

"You are?"

"I figured a week minimum and probably more like two. Detective work, you know? Sneaking around, lurking in the shadows, snooping around for clues. That's a good week right there, and then you still need to find an opportunity to close the deal. What time did you get to Chicago? Eight in the morning?"

"I think it was more like nine."

"That's twelve hours ago."

He looked at his watch. "Twelve and a half."

"I stand corrected. When's your train home, first thing tomorrow morning? Or is there one tonight?"

THERE WAS, BUT he'd missed it. The City of New Orleans left Chicago every evening at 8:05, arriving fifteen and a half hours later at the Loyola Avenue station. They'd probably been calling *All aboard* around the time he pulled into the Super 8 lot.

So he'd made a reservation for the following night, and now he considered his options. There was a Denny's across the street and a Pizza Hut next door on the right, and he stood outside in the cool of the evening and couldn't make a choice. It had taken him maybe thirty seconds to pick the Stanley hammer from the wide array of potential murder weapons, but it was taking him forever to choose between a pizza and a patty melt, and the truth of the matter seemed to be that he didn't want either, or anything else.

But he knew he had to eat, and wound up in a booth at Denny's, further confounded by the array of choices. He picked their Hungry Man's Breakfast, which struck him as curious, given that he didn't feel hungry and nobody but Denny thought it was time for breakfast. The waitress brought him a huge plate of food, and he surprised himself by eating all of it.

Back in his room, he did the mental exercises that always followed a job. Pictured the Marlboro Man as he'd last seen him, slumped over the steering wheel. And then went to work on that picture in the Photoshop of his mind, shrinking it, leaching the color out of it, then working on the tiny black-and-white image he'd made of it, fading it all to gray, shrinking it further until it was a dot, a pinpoint.

He'd taught himself this technique years ago, and for the most part it had proven effective. It wasn't something you did just once, you had to repeat it, but eventually it was difficult to summon up the original image because you really had changed the look of it in your memory.

This time around it was a little hard to get started, because the only image he had to work with didn't start out with much in the way of color or detail. It had been dark by then, and while there were lights in the parking lot, the trio of white vans had been parked well away from them. You'd think it would be easier to blur and shrink and fade an image that wasn't all that vivid to begin with, but for some reason it wasn't.

Well, he did what he could.

AND SLEPT WELL enough, although he awoke with a sense of having been troubled by dreams. He couldn't recall a dream, couldn't even say for certain that he'd been dreaming, but he got out of bed feeling less rested than untroubled sleep should have left him.

He checked out, skipped breakfast, and drove back to O'Hare to return the car. While he was there, he checked the board and saw that United had a flight to Louis Armstrong Airport scheduled to depart at 11:45.

No. Stick with the plan.

He took a cab to the train station, picked up the ticket he'd reserved, and checked his bag. He walked around until he found a place to have coffee, got a croissant while he was at it, and took out his phone. The Pablo phone was in his bag, along with the burner he'd bought and never used, but he was in Chicago now, not Baker's Bluff, and he was Nicholas Edwards once again instead of James J. Miller, so it didn't matter if his iPhone pinged off towers left and right.

He powered it up and called home, and Julia answered.

"I'm in Chicago," he told her. "My train leaves around eight and gets in at three-thirty tomorrow afternoon."

"And everything's taken care of?"

"All wrapped up. I thought it would take longer, but it went well."

"I bet it was the hat. I hope you've still got it."

He lifted a hand, touched the brim to make sure. "I'm wearing it now."

"Well, be careful," she said. "You're in the Windy City."

"That's true."

"Although I read somewhere that they call it that because the local politicians are such windbags, but I don't know if I believe it. If that's how it worked, wouldn't every city be the Windy City?"

HE WALKED AROUND, looked at things, did a little shopping. Ate a meal, saw a movie. They had a lounge in Union Station for first–class passengers, and that's what you became when you booked a roomette. He was in the lounge by 6:30, drinking coffee and watching CNN until they called his train for boarding.

"Good evening, Mr. Edwards. Good to see you again, sir."

It was nice to have the same porter, nicer still that he happened to remember the man's name. "Ainslie," he said, and was rewarded with a smile, while Ainslie was in turn rewarded as before with a twenty-dollar bill.

The dining car wouldn't be serving until breakfast, Ainslie told him, but there'd be coffee and sandwiches in the café car as soon as they got underway. Keller looked out the window for a while, went and had something to eat, and got back to his roomette in time to have Ainslie make up the bed. He lay in the dark for a long time, while the train sped up and slowed down, passing through stations. The last one he was aware of was Centralia, sometime after midnight.

He slept all right, surfacing every couple of hours but lulled back to sleep each time by the motion of the train. After breakfast he called home, but rang off when the call went to voice mail. He was only about a third of the way into Jake Dagger's story, and he'd have returned to it if it hadn't been in his checked bag.

The roomette was supplied with the current issue of Amtrak's magazine, and he read an article proclaiming Richmond, Virginia, as a hot destination for foodies. Keller, a longtime New Yorker now living in New Orleans, was somehow skeptical. He tried to imagine a couple of Tribeca sophisticates, say, or their Vieux Carré equivalents, packing for a weekend of gourmet excess in Richmond. "We'll take the train, darling! Oh, I can hardly wait to dig into that organic kale!"

But what did he know?

HE TRIED JULIA again, rang off when he got a busy signal. Then it was time for lunch, and he had his second meal in the dining car, and called her from his table while he finished his coffee. "Just a couple of hours," he said, and she told him she'd pick him up at the station, but to call her if the train was going to be late. It was on time so far, he said.

"I did a little shopping in Chicago," he added. "I bought Jenny a present."

"Who'd have guessed? You know what I'll do? I'll pick her up from school on my way to the station. That might get me there closer to four than three-thirty."

"That's probably better anyway. I checked my bag, and that means waiting until it makes it to Baggage Claim."

"Oh," she said.

"Oh?"

"Your phone is in your bag."

"No, darling," he said patiently. "It's in my hand. Otherwise we wouldn't be having this conversation."

"The other phone."

"Uh—"

"Dot called a couple of hours ago. She said she couldn't get through to you, and I said reception could be iffy on trains.

She said she'd try again. But if your phone's in your checked luggage—"

"I could call her," he said. "On this phone. But if it's important enough to call her—"

"Then it's important enough to do it on the right phone."

"I'd say so, yes."

"Well, I'll see you in a few hours."

He ended the call, pocketed the phone, and tried to figure out a way that Dot's call could be nothing to worry about. If the client was happy, if he'd sent the rest of the money, she might call him to tell him so. But, failing to reach him, would she call Julia?

No, she wouldn't. So that wasn't it.

While anything might have led her to pick up the Pablo phone, even a simple desire to congratulate him further on a job well done, the second call meant trouble. It indicated not merely that she'd been unable to reach him but that she'd *needed* to reach him, and that wouldn't have been to offer congratulations, or to pass the time of day. Something had gone wrong.

And he'd have to wait to find out what it was. Well, that was okay. He was good at waiting. And this time at least he wouldn't need a wide-mouthed jar.

"THE GOOD NEWS," Dot said, "is that he thinks you did a hell of a job. In that respect he couldn't be happier."

"What's the other respect?"

"I'll get to that, Pablo. First let's look on the bright side, okay?"

The bright side, he thought, was less of a pleasure to look at when you knew the dark side was coming. Still, he focused on it. He was home with his wife and daughter, both of whom seemed happy with what he'd brought them from Chicago. He'd done his work quickly and efficiently, and to the evident satisfaction of his employer. And now he was in his stamp room, talking on a safe phone with his best friend of many years standing. If there was bad news to come, he figured he could handle it.

"What I had to do," Dot said, "is make it clear we'd done the job without telling him the name of the guy we'd done it on."

"Because we didn't know it."

"And because it's safer if he doesn't know it, either. So what I did, I gave him a play-by-play of your investigation."

"Oh?"

"I left out the wide-mouthed jar," she said, "and the fedora. I told him you parked where you could keep an eye on the house, and at such-and-such a time the garage door opened, and a white van pulled in right next to the subject's Lexus, and—"

"The subject?"

"That would be his wife, Pablo. Remember her?"

"Vividly. It was the word I was reacting to. 'The subject.'"

"I was reporting to a client. I figured it was more businesslike to say 'the subject's Lexus' than 'that overpriced Japanese import you bought for your whore of a wife.' May I continue?"

"Sorry."

"I called the guy who got out of the van the unsub. That stands for—"

"Unidentified Subject."

"I guess we watch the same TV shows. Other hand, Overmont must stick to PBS and the History Channel, because I had to translate the term for him. Anyway, Unsub exits vehicle, female subject meets and embraces him—"

"That didn't happen," he said. "Well, it probably did, but I never observed it."

"I was embroidering, Pablo. Improving on the truth. The rest of it was straightforward enough. They're in the house for whatever it was, half an hour, an hour, and then there's another kiss and hug and a little canoodling as he gets in the van and drives off, and don't tell me it didn't happen, or that you didn't see it, okay? I wanted to leave no doubt in his mind, and since you're the only person who can swear you didn't see it—"

"I get the point."

"Well, good. Then you followed in close pursuit, and took your opportunity when it presented itself, bringing the proceedings to a satisfactory and permanent conclusion. You see what I did, Pablo? Lots of details early on, enough to sink the hook, and then nothing specific—no name, no location, no details on what you did or how you did it."

"That was really clever of you."

"That's what I thought," she said. "Turns out we were both wrong."

"How do you figure that?"

"What I did," she said, "is I drew him a blueprint. And what he did, the son of a bitch, is he followed it."

"I GUESS HE was all excited," he told Julia. "His rival was out of the picture, and his wife didn't even know it, and he decided to celebrate his victory. So what he did, he left his office early and went home."

"To Baker's Bluff?"

"That's right. He figured his wife would be home, waiting for her boyfriend, and instead of a man in a van she'd get a husband in a Mercedes."

"It doesn't rhyme," she said.

"Not many things rhyme with husband. Or Mercedes, as far as that goes."

"Hades, ladies, Rosie O'Grady's. Nothing useful. Does he have children from a prior marriage? He could be a daddy in a Caddy, if you could get him to trade in the Mercedes. I'm sorry, I'm not letting you finish."

"You're not the only one. What he did, he drove home, got there around three in the afternoon. And he parked across the street, because he was on the early side, and he thought he'd give her a little time to wonder what happened to her lover."

"And then what? 'Ha ha, guess who's not coming over?'"

"That would have been really stupid," he said, "although I'd say it's not out of the question. But we'll never know what he would have done, because while he was waiting, you'll never guess what happened."

"The garage door opened."

"Good guess."

"And she backed out? No, somebody came in. Was he alive? The Marlboro Man?"

"The garage door went up," he said, "just as a white van turned into the driveway."

"Omigod. You smacked him twice with a hammer. He must have had a head made of cast iron."

"And then—"

"To say nothing of his sex drive," she went on, "and her irresistible animal magnetism, drawing him back from the brink of death. I'm sorry, I keep interrupting. What happened next? The garage door closed?"

He shook his head. "The door of the house opened," he said, "and she came out, Melania, and the two of them met. And no, it wasn't the Marlboro Man."

"She gets around, this lady."

"She does. The two of them met somewhere between his van and her door, and they talked, and Todd sat in his car and watched. And then they went into the house and the door closed, and a little later the garage door closed, too, and nothing happened for three quarters of an hour."

"Nothing happened?"

"Well, nothing you could see from a Mercedes-Benz parked across the street. But he could certainly use his imagination."

"And he waited there, like a good detective. Even if he didn't have a fedora."

"What he probably missed more was a wide-mouthed jar. Yes, he waited, and then the door opened and they walked out together, and I gather it was all he could do to stay where he was."

"And she didn't spot him? I mean, she'd recognize the car, wouldn't she?"

"Only if she looked at it, and she only had eyes for the guy."

"Who was not the Marlboro Man."

"No, but he was definitely her type."

"In that he had a Y chromosome?"

"Big, broad-shouldered, muscular. The two of them put on a little kiss-kiss show for the husband, and then Melania went back into the house and the guy got in his van and drove off."

"And the husband followed him."

"Tried to. Lost him almost immediately."

"But I suppose he got the license plate number."

"You'd think so, wouldn't you?"

"He didn't?"

"Dot said he thinks there was a seven in it, but she may have made that up."

She thought that over. At length she said, "If he thinks he deserves a refund—"

"No, he's satisfied I did my job."

"But she's still got a lover, so he's still got a problem. Don't tell me he wants you to solve it."

"He wants someone to solve it. I'm not sure he cares who it is. But he only knows one number to call, and he called it."

"And got Dot. And what does she want?"

"What she wanted," he said, "was to confirm that as far as I was concerned we were done. She'd tell him something—too risky to go back, the agent's already booked through September, di dah di dah di dah. In other words thanks but no thanks, and anyway your wife's the problem, and if big brawny guys stop showing up in vans, she'll make do with skinny kids pushing grocery carts."

"Because she's a whore, and he should either leave her or live with it."

"Exactly."

"So you told her yes, go ahead and tell him that." She looked at him. "Except you didn't, did you?"

"I probably should have," he admitted.

"But you didn't."

"I didn't, no."

"You're going back," she said.

"Not right away. I want to spend the rest of this week right here, and come Sunday I want to take Jenny to the zoo."

"To make sure the alligator is still dead. And Monday you go back to Chicago?"

"Monday or Tuesday. There's no big rush."

"And you'll go through all that again? Waiting for the new Marlboro Man to show up so you can follow him?" Her eyes narrowed. "No," she said. "You won't have to do that, will you?"

"Not this time."

"So you can leave the fedora home. That's good, I wouldn't want anything to happen to it. I don't suppose you'll need the jar, either. What happened to the jar?"

"I left it in the rental car."

"Well, if the next person they give it to is a detective, I'm sure he'll appreciate it. You don't have to do a stakeout this time because you know who it is, don't you? But how can you know?"

"From the husband's description," he said.

"Big, broad-shouldered, and muscular."

"Plus a detail Dot almost didn't mention, because she didn't realize the significance. He was wearing boots."

"So?"

"Western-style boots," he said. "And a cowboy hat."

IT WAS TUESDAY afternoon when he boarded the City of New Orleans, and no great surprise when Ainslie greeted him by name and gratefully accepted the customary twenty dollars. This time Keller had remembered to check his bag, but had held onto both his iPhone and the Pablo phone, along with something to read. He'd thought it might feel strange to be back on the train again, but all it felt was familiar, as if this was something he did all the time. Which, in a sense, it was.

He drank a cup of coffee, he looked out the window, he read for a while. He went to the diner and found something to order on the menu he'd long since memorized; back in his roomette, he had brief conversations with Julia and Jenny on the iPhone, and with Dot on the Pablo phone, and around ten he summoned Ainslie to make up the bed.

He slept deeply, and when he came back from breakfast Ainslie told him they were running late. "We were right on schedule," he reported. "Got into Homewood at twenty minutes of eight, which made us a couple of minutes early, and then they held us there with no explanation, and now it looks like we'll be an hour late getting to Chicago. I just hope you don't have an early appointment."

"No, I'm in no rush," he said.

"Well, I'm glad to hear that, Mr. Edwards. I can now tell you the delay had nothing to do with *this* train. There was a south-bound freight train way up ahead of us, not even on our track as it was heading south and we were heading north—"

"So it's good it was on the other track."

"Yes sir, you're right about that. But don't you know a fool in a white van went around the barrier? Now he's dead, and the man driving that freight train's got a few bad weeks in front of him, plus the nightmares he's sure to be having. And all of us in another train entirely are an hour late getting to Chicago."

"He wasn't wearing a cowboy hat, was he?"

"How's that, Mr. Edwards?"

"Oh, it's nothing, Ainslie. Just thinking out loud."

HE PICKED UP his suitcase at Baggage Claim, caught a cab to O'Hare. Hertz had a car ready for him, and it was a Subaru like the one he'd had before. That did make it easier, it saved the hour or so you spent flicking on the lights when you were trying to signal a left turn. And he knew how to adjust the seat to his liking, and cope with the GPS.

Not that he really needed the GPS. He'd driven the route too recently to have forgotten it. Still, he set the thing, and let the woman's voice give him a head's-up half a mile before each turn. It was reassuring to know that, should his mind wander, she was there to keep him on the right track.

He drove straight to the Super 8, where they had a room for Mr. Miller. It was a different room from last time, still on the ground floor but at the opposite end of the building, but it ceased being different when he opened the door to a unit that was identical to the one he'd had before. Which was inevitable, he supposed, because it was a Super 8 Motel, and the units were pretty much identical all over the country. It certainly stood to reason that two rooms in a particular motel would be indistinguishable one from the other. The same layout, the same furnishings, the same configuration in the bathroom, the same notice about throwing the towels on the floor to save water, or whatever their reason was for wanting you to do it. He was fairly certain global warming came into the picture somewhere.

Still, it gave him a turn.

IF YOU DIDN'T mind getting your picture taken, you could buy just about anything at Walmart.

They had security cameras all over the place, both inside and outside the enormous store, and that was almost reason enough for Keller to go someplace else. But where could you go without leaving a photographic record? There were security cameras in his motel, and in its parking lot. More Americans had starring roles on closed-circuit TV than appeared in YouTube videos, and from what he'd read it was even worse in England, where an unrecorded moment outside one's own home had become a rare thing indeed.

But an unsolved crime, here or in the UK, was less of a rarity, so Keller wasn't sure the cameras made all that much of a difference. And the footage—did you even call it that when it was digital?—well, whatever you called it, they'd need a reason to look at it, wouldn't they? Something that lingered in a clerk's memory, something recorded that triggered suspicions.

Say you wheeled your cart to the checkout counter, and the only item in it was a wicked-looking Bowie knife with a nine-inch blade. Say the clerk pointed out that they had whetstones in Aisle

Fourteen, and you said you figured it was sharp enough as it was, and you were only planning to use it once.

"A gun would be better," you could add, "if it weren't for that darned waiting period."

Keller, wheeling his cart, chose a print, matted and framed, of two kittens worrying a ball of yarn. Two aisles over he found picture hooks, and a three-foot coil of picture-hanging wire.

Next stop, hammers. The one he picked struck him as identical to the one he'd found in the Marlboro Man's van, and felt very much the same in his hand. The same weight, the same good balance, the same black rubber easy-grip handle.

"That's so *sweet!*" the checkout clerk said, holding the print at arm's length. "For your daughter's room?"

"My niece," Keller said.

"Well, I know she'll love it."

She gave him two shopping bags—the framed print got one all to itself—and he carried them to the car. Half a mile away he parked at a strip mall, and added the picture hooks and the wire to the bag with the print, depositing the lot in a trash can.

He drove off with the hammer on the seat beside him.

Why had he bothered to correct the woman? Why insist the picture was for his niece and not his daughter?

Because, he thought, he didn't have a niece. He had a daughter, and was more comfortable leaving her out of it. And he could picture Julia's face if he'd tried hanging the kitten print in Jenny's room. She'd be happier with a dead alligator.

It occurred to him that the discarded picture wire would have been easy to fashion into a garrote. But that would have been the last thing he'd want for the scenario he had in mind. A garrote, simple enough to prepare, nevertheless required preparation. You didn't have a sudden flare-up of fury and reach for a piece of picture wire. You needed time, and you probably needed a certain degree of professionalism in the bargain—to make it, in the first place, and then to employ it effectively. The garrote was not the weapon of an amateur.

At a stoplight, he reached over and rested a hand on the hammer. His only tool, he thought. Now to go find himself a nail.

※

SOMETHING MADE HIM drive by the Overmont house. He didn't park, and barely slowed down, and all he saw was the house itself. The garage door was closed, as it always seemed to be unless someone was on the way in or out, and there were no cars parked in the driveway or on the street nearby.

He drove off, wondering what he had hoped to see. "I told him what he ought to do was get out of town," Dot had reported earlier. "Take his wife, fly off for a few fun-filled days in Las Vegas or Cancún or, hell, I don't know. Where do people like that go?"

"People like what?"

"Nymphomaniacs," she said, "and the morons who love them. I'd love to get them both out of town, but I'm not counting on it."

"Just so he quits playing detective."

"Oh, there'll be no more of that," she said. "No more leaving the office early, no more surprise visits."

That was something.

※

THERE WERE TWO white vans parked at the Wet Spot, and his first thought was that they were both here, Cowboy Hat and Tom Cruise. The vans weren't parked side by side, and he saw right away that both were parked much nearer to the building than the original group of three had been, but it took a closer look than that to establish that these weren't the vehicles he was looking for.

Both bore lettering on their doors, one proclaiming itself the property of a boiler repair firm, the other showing a pink pig wearing a top hat and carrying a cane. It might have been interesting to speculate as to what the Pig About Town was selling, and there was a phone number under the logo that he could have called, but they weren't the vans he was looking for, and that was really as much as he needed to know.

What was the other place?

The Spotted Tiger, and he couldn't remember what street it was on. He could go into the Wet Spot and ask, and somebody would be sure to know, but maybe the GPS would tell him.

He tried, and it did. Spotted Tiger Restaurant, 3304 Quincy Avenue. That sounded right, Quincy, and anyway, how right did it have to sound? I mean, how many Spotted Tigers were there likely to be?

☀

FROM THE OUTSIDE, the Spotted Tiger looked a lot like the Wet Spot. No white vans, though, which surprised Keller. You'd think they'd have one or two parked there, even if they weren't the one he was looking for.

He went inside, just to make sure, and it was the right kind of crowd, too, a roomful of rednecks raising their voices to make themselves heard over a jukebox on which Marty Robbins was singing about the West Texas town of El Paso. Keller ordered a beer and looked around the room, while his mind tried to think of words to rhyme with El Paso. He right away came up with lasso, and that was as far as he got.

He saw a lot of men wearing boots, and even a Stetson or two, but he didn't see Tom Cruise's stunt double, and neither did he see the Marlboro Man's near-twin.

He had a sip of beer. Well, he'd confirmed it. Their vans weren't here and neither were they, and one sip was as much beer as he wanted to put in his system. He'd put a twenty on the bar, and now he scooped up enough of his change to leave an appropriate tip, and realized that he was thinking about eels, and how he'd read somewhere that all the eels in the world were born in the same spot, and they then went their separate ways, returning to wherever their parents had come from, and then when their lives had run their natural course, they somehow knew to swim back halfway across the world to where they'd been hatched. Where they would spawn and, with what Keller imagined was a great sense of relief, expire.

Was that even true? Never mind how he knew it, because he didn't really *know* it, he'd just heard it or read it somewhere. Was it really every eel, or just a particular species? And how could anyone know for sure? Even if they tagged the mama and papa eels, so they knew they'd all gone to the same place, how would they know which little elvers had which parents?

But that, he realized, was the least of it. What was baffling was why this particular thought came to his mind just now, when he had no reason to think of eels or elvers or their ancestral home in the Sargasso Sea.

Oh.

El Paso, lasso, and Sargasso.

He'd thought he'd forgotten all about Marty Robbins and the damn song, but evidently he hadn't, and there it was, running around in his mind even when his mind was turned off. The song had long since ended, he'd only heard the last half-minute of it, and a couple of songs had played since to which he'd paid no attention.

Well, no conscious attention, because God knows what his mind was capable of when he wasn't tuned in. A couple of songs, and he didn't even know what they were, and right now Johnny Cash was telling everybody how he walked the line, and all of a sudden it seemed important to find out what the songwriter had rhymed with El Paso. It couldn't be Sargasso, could it? Lasso was possible, in that kind of Old West song, but—

Oh, hell. He'd left his coins on the bar, along with a couple of singles, but he picked up a couple of quarters and found his way over to the juke box. There it was, B-17, Marty Robbins, "El Paso." He paid fifty cents to play it, which struck him as silly, considering that YouTube would happily let him hear it for free in the privacy of his own home.

And then he went back to his bar stool and waited while other people's selections got played ahead of his. Loretta Lynn and Bobby Bare and Crystal Gayle, and a few he didn't recognize, and he was beginning to understand how every once in a while you read about somebody in a place like this who took out a gun and started blasting away at the juke box. He'd always figured it was because they couldn't stand the song that was playing, but maybe they couldn't stand the song that *wasn't* playing.

Ah, finally! *Down in the West Texas town of El Paso...*

Without thinking, he'd picked up his beer and taken an unintended sip of it.

Not that a sip of beer would hurt him any. Still, it was bothersome that he'd done it after deciding not to. And he couldn't afford to think about it, not now, because his song was playing, and he had to listen closely to find out what rhymed with El Paso.

Nothing, as it turned out.

The name of the song was El Paso, and it turned up in the lyrics a couple of times, and always at the end of a line. So you couldn't think of the song without thinking of the town, but that didn't mean that there was anything in there to rhyme with it. It came at the end of the first line in a stanza, and the rhymes were the words at the ends of lines two and four. So what rhymed with El Paso?

"Not a goddamned thing," he said.

"Pardner," a voice said at his elbow, "I have to say you got that right."

AND, OF COURSE, the man standing just to his right, the man who'd agreed with him without knowing what it was he was agreeing with, was big and tall and broad in the shoulders. And, no surprise, he was wearing boots. And, duh, a cowboy hat.

Keller, who hadn't realized he'd spoken out loud, now had the opportunity to wish he hadn't. While he was at it, he wished he'd saved fifty cents and ten or twelve minutes and left the Spotted Tiger while he had the chance.

"Um," he said. "I don't think we know each other."

"Hell, I know you," Cowboy Hat said. He turned to the shorter fellow on his right, who unsurprisingly turned out to be Tom Cruise. "Hey, Pete," he said. "Remember this fellow?"

"Can't say I do," said Tom Cruise, whose name was evidently Pete.

"I can believe it, drunk as you was." He shook his head, turned to Keller. "Last week," he said. "We was right here, and you was right there. Except we was all three of us in the Wet Spot, not here in the Tiger. But you, you didn't say a word, just drank your beer like a gentleman, and one minute you was there and the next minute you was gone."

"Well," Keller said.

"Is it coming back to you now, Pete?"

"Nope."

"See, that's the difference between you and me. I'm a man never forgets a face."

"Can't say the same," Pete admitted. "Now I got a memory for vehicles. Show me a car, I'll say, 'Damn, I seen that car before.' Unless I didn't, in which case I won't."

"You and your cars," Cowboy Hat said. "How about hats, little buddy? You got any kind of a memory for hats?"

"I remember yours," Pete said. "I ought to, I seen that ugly thing enough times."

"Last time you saw this here gentleman, that you can't remember ever seeing before, he was wearing one of the nicest looking hats you'll ever hope to see." He laid a hand on Keller's shoulder. "What happened to that hat, pardner?"

"Uh," Keller said.

"Nice gray felt hat, had a little turned-down brim, little crease right here—" he ran an illustrative forefinger along the top of Keller's head "—and dimples here—" he used his thumb and forefinger to give a light pinch to Keller's forehead. "There's a name for that kind of hat, but I disremember what it is."

"A fedora," Keller murmured.

"Say again? Couldn't quite hear you, what with all the noise in this place."

"A fedora."

"Yep, that's it. Had it right on the tip of my tongue. A fedora." He heaved a sigh, stuck out his hand. "Roy Savage," he said.

"Jim," Keller said, and shook Roy's hand.

"And this here's Pete, though it's a waste of time introducing you, on account of he won't remember."

Another solemn handshake, with Pete assuring his new friend Jim that he'd sure remember him. "And your car, too," he added.

Wonderful, just wonderful.

THE LAST THING Keller ever wanted to do was get acquainted with the subject of an assignment. All he liked to have, really, was enough information so he could make a positive identification of the intended target. That often entailed knowing his name, but it was even better if he didn't. It might not have made it more difficult to swing a hammer into the temple of the Marlboro Man if he'd known his name was Harold, but neither would it have made it easier.

It was Cowboy Hat—no, dammit, make that Roy—who supplied the name. Harold Garber, he said, after they'd all moved from the bar to a table, where Roy said they'd be able to hear better. Keller didn't want to hear better, he didn't want to hear anything at all, but he couldn't figure out a way to leave that wouldn't be even more memorable than if he were to stay.

Hell.

"Old Harold," he said. "Man couldn't ask for a better friend."

"And look what you done," Pete said.

"What?"

"Before Harold was even in the ground," he said, "you was hitting on the widow."

"Widow? Harold wasn't married."

"No, but *she* was," Pete said. "Jim, you remember when we was in here that night? You was wearing your hat. And I remember that hat, matter of fact. Remember it perfectly well."

Well, that was a comfort.

"I don't remember all that much myself," Keller volunteered.

"Harold couldn't stop talking about this babe he spent the afternoon with," Pete said. "And then the next thing we heard was Harold was dead. Killed right there in the parking lot at the Wet Spot, found dead in his truck with his head bashed in."

Keller said that was terrible.

"With his own hammer," Roy said, "which they called a crime of opportunity. You all of a sudden decide to kill a man, you look around for something, and there's his hammer. Wham, and it's done."

"And Roy here was so shocked," Pete said, "that the first chance he gets he's over at the house on Robin's Nest Road comforting the widow."

"You are so wrong."

"Oh yeah?"

"First of all, it's Robin's Nest Drive, not Road."

"You look up Same Fucking Difference in the dictionary, what do you suppose you're gonna see?"

"And on top of that, she wasn't anybody's widow, on account of her husband's still alive. And that's why I went there, you moron."

"Because you're a hound is why."

"I was being considerate," he said, and turned to Keller for support. "You'd do the same thing, right?"

"Uh—"

"Okay, bringing you up to speed. Harold had this girlfriend, rich lady, husband, old story. Saw her and didn't exactly keep it to hisself."

"'Smell my finger,'" Pete said.

"Liked to boast a bit," Roy said, "but who's he hurting? None of us knows the woman."

"One of us does now."

"Pete, shut up, okay? Point is Harold died sudden."

"On account of somebody killed him."

"Followed him out the door and back to his van," Roy said. "That's what happened, most likely. There's Harold, boasting the way he'd do, and there's a roomful of men can't help overhearing him—"

"On account of he'd raise his voice to make damn sure they heard him."

"Well, that was Harold, all right. And I'm a little fuzzy on the details, I had a few beers myself, but we all of us decided to get out of there and come to the Tiger instead."

"Too many tattoos," Pete said.

"Anyway, Pete here took off."

"Drove from there to here," Pete said. "Nothing to it."

"And I figured to let Harold go next, and I'd bring up the rear, but what happened was he was waiting for me to go, so it was like the two Frenchies. What's their damn names, Pete?"

"Frenchies?"

"You know. 'After you, my friend.' 'No, after you!' Couple of Froggies, and what are their damn names?"

"Only Frenchman I know is that guy Giuseppe, and he's Italian."

"You're a big help, Pete."

Alphonse and Gaston, Keller thought, but kept it to himself.

"Pierre," Roy said, "and Lucky Pierre. That's not it, but it'll do. So I headed for the Tiger, and Pete was already here when I pulled in."

"Took you long enough," Pete said.

"And we waited for Harold, and when we got tired of waiting we went in and had a couple of beers. And it wasn't until the next day that we heard what happened to Harold."

"He got hammered," Pete offered.

"We all got hammered," Roy said, "but with Harold it wasn't just an expression. Guy followed him out, had to be a case of Harold got it on with somebody's wife or girlfriend—"

"Or daughter."

"Yeah, coulda been a daughter. Cops are working their way through the Wet Spot's regulars, checking out everybody that mighta had it in for Harold."

Keller half-listened while the two of them worked their way through a lengthy list of potential suspects. Earlier, he'd remembered a job years ago that had sent him across the country to a town in Oregon, where someone had spotted a man who'd vanished into the Witness Protection Program. Keller liked the place, liked the life the man was leading there, and found himself contemplating retirement. It was just a fantasy, but in the course of it he'd made the horrible mistake of getting to know the fellow.

When, inevitably, he'd come to his senses, his mission was consequently far more difficult. Still, you did what you had to do. But, having done it, you took pains to avoid such complications in the future.

As Roy went on and on, now explaining how he'd known it was his duty to tell this woman on Robin's Nest Drive what had happened to Harold, because otherwise she might never know, or she'd read it in the paper, or worst of all the police would turn up on her doorstep and give her the shock of her life, and—

On and on and on, with Pete chiming in now and then, and with Roy admitting that, well, he had to admit he'd wanted to confirm some of the things Harold had told him about the lady, because Harold had a tendency to exaggerate, but in this instance Harold had it right, all right, and—

All of this, he realized, was very different from what he'd gone through in Roseburg, Oregon. There he'd liked the man, and he'd had to set that aside and do his job. But here in Baker's Bluff, the more time he spent with Roy and his friend Pete, the fewer his reservations about earning his fee. Every sentence spoken, every clap of that big hand on his shoulder, made Keller a little more eager to swing that brand-new Stanley hammer not merely with professionalism but with pleasure.

And now, of course, it was out of the question.

"BACK IN A minute," he said. "I want to hear the rest of this."

He got to his feet. Roy was in the middle of a sentence, but Roy was pretty much always in the middle of a sentence, and a call of nature was something a beer drinker could certainly understand. Keller went to the restroom, answered nature's call, and left the room.

Back in a minute. I want to hear the rest of this.

Well, how was that for a pair of barefaced lies, one right after the other? He certainly didn't want to hear anymore, nor would he be back, not in a minute and not in an hour. He walked out of the men's room and down the hall and out the door, took a quick backward glance to make sure no one was paying attention, and crossed the lot to his car.

He got behind the wheel, stuck the key in the ignition, and looked over at the passenger seat, where the hammer was waiting. He shouldn't have bought the hammer, he thought. For that matter, he shouldn't have bought that second ticket to Chicago. He should have stayed home.

He got out the Pablo phone, made a call.

"I can't do anything," he said. "I bought a hammer, it's on the car seat next to me, perfectly good hammer, never been used—and all I can do is toss it."

"If you toss it far enough," Dot said, "you could wind up with an Olympic medal."

"I think that's a different kind of hammer."

"You're probably right. What happened?"

He told her.

"I get it," she said. "You got to know them, and you bonded a little, and the idea of taking them out—"

"—is more appealing than ever," he said, "because not even Krazy Glue could bond me to these two idiots. But I've been seen with them, and in a public place, and—"

"And if anything happens to either of them, somebody's going to remember their friend with the hammer."

"And come looking," he said.

"I'll tell the client," she said. "And I'll send the money back."

"He paid?"

"In full for the original job, which he won't get back because we fulfilled the contract. But he sent half the payment for your friend in the cowboy hat, and—"

"Not my friend."

"It's just an expression, Pablo. He sent half by FedEx, and I'll send it back to him. God, how I hate to return money."

"I know."

"Once I actually have it in hand, you know, it's not their money anymore. So why should they get it back?"

Wait a minute…

"Dot—"

"Oh, I know why. I'm talking about how my mind works. But, you know, that's just my mind, and I've learned not to pay too much attention to it. I'll send the money back."

"Not just yet," he said.

"Oh?"

"I just thought of something."

He retrieved his key, opened the door. He paused for another glance at the passenger seat, wishing the fedora were sitting there. But no, all that was there was the hammer, and he had no use for it now.

BACK IN THE Spotted Tiger, he stopped at the bar for three bottles of beer and carried them back to the table. "Well now," Roy said appreciatively. "Thanks, pardner. Pete, we're drinking to the man with the hat."

Keller took a hearty sip of beer, acknowledging the toast. It struck him as curious, given that he was the only bareheaded man at the table, but it seemed to confirm what the salesman at Peller & Smythe had said about the classic quality of the fedora. It continued to impress people even when you were no longer wearing it.

"Something I was thinking," he said. "Maybe I'm remembering wrong, but didn't you ask your friend, the one who got killed—"

"Harold," Pete supplied.

"Right, Harold. Didn't you ask him if the lady had a sister?"

"Well, you know," Roy said. "Sort of joking with him. Seems to me he said she was an only child."

"But wasn't there was something about how he thought she'd be up for a threesome?"

Roy got a look on his face.

Pete: "Hey, look who swallowed the canary!"

Roy: "No such thing."

Pete: "Where'd that canary-eating grin come from? There's something you ain't telling."

Roy: "Well—"

Well, Roy explained, he was going to mention it. Because he'd actually brought up the subject to Melania, and the last thing she wanted was anything that involved another woman. Anything that went down in her life, she wanted to be the only girl in the room.

"But a second guy," he said, "might be different. And I was gonna say something, but, well, two guys is one thing and three guys is another, and—"

Keller held up a hand, palm forward. "You know what they say," he said. "Four is a crowd. And I'm leaving town first thing in the morning, won't be back for close to three weeks."

Pete wanted to know where he was going, and that required some swift improvisation. Keller invented a trip to San Francisco, and Roy said he'd always wanted to go there, and Pete said he'd heard it was cold in the summer, so why would anyone want to go there?

Keller picked up his beer bottle and drank deep. He wasn't working, there wouldn't be any work for him, so why not enjoy the beer? And drinking it was something to do while he waited for the conversation to get back on track.

"So I can't," he said, when he got the chance. "But the two of you—"

Pete: "Yeah. Like how about tomorrow?"

Roy: "Well, I can't just drop in, say 'Here's my friend,' he wants to join the party."

Keller: "Maybe if you called her…"

Pete: "Yeah! Call her!"

Roy: "And when her husband answers?"

Pete: "So you hang up. But if *she's* the one who answers…"

Roy squinted, thinking about it. He said, "Two on one. Something else they call it, but what is it?"

"Threesomes," Pete said, helpfully. "Threesome, three-way."

"No, when it's two men and one lady." He snapped his fingers. "Tag team!"

"Ever done that?"

Pete shook his head.

"Me neither. Jim?"

It was, for a change, a question Keller could answer honestly. "Never," he said.

Pete: "When you think about, you know, the possibilities…"

Roy, who seemed to be thinking about the possibilities, drew a deep breath and got to his feet, cell phone in hand. "Y'all give me a minute," he said.

ROY CAME BACK with another round of beers, and news that the phone call had been a success. "Quarter past three tomorrow afternoon," he announced. "We'll meet up and take my van, 'cause there's only room for one vehicle in her garage."

Was that double entendre? Keller decided it wasn't.

"What we don't want to be is late," Roy went on, "on account of we want to take our time. Husband's got a long drive home after a full day at the office, but he could walk in anytime after six."

"And what was it Jim here said? 'Four's a crowd.'"

"I'd say the two of us could handle him, but I'd just as soon not have to."

"Rather spend my time handling her," Pete said. "Damn, man, you went and talked her into it!"

Roy beamed, but Keller sensed that it hadn't been that hard a sell. More like persuading a bee to sip nectar, or coaxing a moth toward a flame.

Pete said, "You're the man, man. Old Harold, you figure he would have shared?"

"I'd say no. Harold, he was a hell of a guy, but I can't say he was much of a one for sharing. Let me borrow his van one time, and first I had to sit through a whole lecture on how to keep from grinding the gears."

"You want to grind her gears tomorrow, buddy, I'd say go right ahead."

"Hey, no worry there, Pete. This particular model's self-lubricating."

Oh, spare me, Keller thought. He said, "Two hours and change should be plenty of time. I mean, you won't have to invest a lot of time in small talk."

"No," Roy said, "have to say she's good to go."

He nodded. "Of course," he said, "it'd be good to be prepared just in case. Suppose he comes home early and he's got something in his hand."

"A hammer," Pete said.

They looked at him.

"Guy like that," he explained, "guy that owns his own home, you know he's got a work bench with a few hundred tools on it."

"Right," Roy said. "Son of a bitch could walk into the bedroom carrying a spirit level."

"I'm just saying—"

"Or a measuring tape," Roy said, "in case there's anything Melania doesn't get around to measuring."

"I said a hammer because I was thinking about Harold is all."

Right, Keller thought. "What *I* was thinking," he said, "is if I was coming to that party tomorrow, I'd think about bringing a gun."

"Harold had one," Roy said.

He did?

"And a whole lot of good it did him," Pete said. "Guy sneaks up behind you, your head's caved in before you can even think about getting that old gun off your hip."

"And it's no use unless you've got it in your hand," Roy said. "But you're right, pardner." He patted his hip. "I won't have to remember. Never leave home without it, you know?"

A FEW MINUTES later Keller had a genuine reason to visit the restroom, and decided he didn't need to return to the table. He slipped outside, went to his car.

So the Marlboro Man had had a gun on his hip? He hadn't known that, and it struck him as the sort of thing one would want to know in advance. Then again, he hadn't suspected Cowboy Roy was walking around strapped, and that could have posed a real problem, especially if the scenario had called for him to deal with Roy and Pete at the same time. There were far too many ways that could have gone wrong, and just thinking about them was sobering.

Speaking of which, he wondered if he was okay to drive. He'd had what, three beers? And a sip of a fourth? He thought about it and decided he felt clearheaded enough. And once he got underway he certainly seemed to be fine, listening to the gentle but firm voice of the GPS lady, and following her instructions all the way back to the Super 8.

"I GOT RID of the hammer," he told Dot. "Brand new hammer and I tossed it in a trash can."

"You could have taken it back for a refund," she said, "but what would you do, tell them it didn't work? 'Sir, you're supposed to hold it by the handle, not the head.' How far away was the trash can?"

"I was standing right next to it. It wasn't a toss, really. I just dropped it in."

"Well, nobody's gonna give you a medal for that. So now should I send the money back?"

"Maybe wait a day," he said.

HE PUT THE Pablo phone away, took out his iPhone, decided he didn't care if it pinged off towers in Baker's Bluff. What difference did it make now? He called Amtrak and booked a roomette on the City of New Orleans for the following night, then called Julia and told her he'd be home the day after that.

"I'll pick you up at the station," she said. "It, uh, went okay?"

"I sort of called it off."

"I'm glad, if it means you're getting on a train tomorrow night. Still, it's a shame. Not that you called it off, but that you made the trip for nothing."

"Well," he said. "That remains to be seen."

∼⧸⧹∽

HE SLEPT UNTIL he woke up, then checked out of his motel and drove across the street to Denny's. Something made him follow the GPS prompts to Robin's Nest Drive, and all that accomplished was confirmation that the Overmont house was still standing. It had not burned to the foundation, or been swept away in a flash flood, or imploded from emotional intensity. The garage door was closed, the drapes were drawn, and not a single vehicle was parked at the curb for the full length of the block.

Was there any reason to look more closely? Any reason to do anything at all in the pleasant town of Baker's Bluff?

None that he could think of. He touched the GPS screen, selected Previous Destinations, and headed for O'Hare to give the car back to Hertz.

∼⧸⧹∽

AND FROM THERE to Chicago, where James J. Miller of Waco went back to being Nicholas Edwards of New Orleans. It wasn't noon yet, and his train wasn't scheduled to leave until 8:05, so after he'd picked up the ticket he'd reserved and used it to check his bag through to New Orleans, he had a whole day to kill.

Well, he thought, maybe that wasn't the best choice of words.

He'd put his three phones in three different pockets before he checked his bag, and now he found a quiet corner in Amtrak's Metropolitan Lounge. He examined all three phones in turn, and decided there was really only one call he had to make, and only one phone on which to make it.

It rang three times before it was answered, and the fellow on the other end managed to put a world of uncertainty into the single word *hello*.

"You don't know me," Keller said. "But there's something you really need to know, and something you really ought to do about it."

⌁

WHEN HE LIVED in New York, a stone's throw from the United Nations, Keller had done a minimal amount of decorating. The bedroom held a couple of inoffensive Japanese prints. He'd never paid much attention to them, and at this point he couldn't begin to remember what they'd looked like.

But in the living room he'd hung a framed poster he'd picked up at the Whitney. There'd been an Edward Hopper retrospective, and one painting after another had caught him and held him, although it would have been hard for him to say why. The hold was sufficient to prompt him to buy the poster, and it still worked when he brought it home and hung it on the wall.

It was *Nighthawks*, perhaps the artist's most iconic work, and while it had been on loan to the Whitney when he saw it, he seemed to remember that its actual home was a museum in Chicago. His iPhone Google app confirmed this, and a cab took him to the front steps of the Art Institute, and in no time at all he was standing in front of the painting, looking at the three customers in the diner.

He stood there, drinking it in. It had been a few years now since a trip to Des Moines left him framed for a political assassination, and that was the end of his residence in New York. Of all the apartment's contents, only his stamp collection remained in his possession, and only because Dot had rushed to retrieve it.

Had he seen a reproduction of *Nighthawks* since then? He could have, it was reproduced frequently, and he might have run across it when browsing the internet, but he couldn't specifically recall such an occasion. And yet the painting was as vivid in his memory as if he'd looked at it yesterday, and had the emotional impact upon him that it had the first time he stood in front of it.

He found it cheering, actually. Loneliness, it assured him, was the human condition. It hadn't singled him out.

Both male customers, he noted, were wearing fedoras.

HE WAS SETTLED in the lounge a little after six, and thought about hauling out the burner phone and trying the number again. But to what end?

In fact, wasn't it dangerous to have the phone on his person? He'd powered it down after making the single call on it, so it wouldn't be doing any pinging, but simply continuing to own it might be a bad idea. A storm drain was a logical destination for it, but he'd have to leave Union Station to find one, and that seemed like more trouble than it was worth.

The safest thing to do, he thought, was to smash the thing. But for that he'd need a hammer, and the one he'd bought was in a trash can at the Super 8.

You're overthinking this, he told himself, and headed for the lounge's restroom, then overthought that as well and left the lounge long enough to visit a public restroom on the other side of the concourse. There he balanced the phone on top of the paper towel dispenser, where someone could adopt it, use up its remaining minutes, and find his own storm drain.

࿇

AFTER THE RITUAL preliminaries ("Mr. Edwards, a pleasure to see you, sir!" "Oh, am I in your car, Ainslie? Then I know I'm in good hands.") and the ritual passing of the twenty-dollar bill, Ainslie said, "Now I was just about to ask what had become of that fine hat of yours, and then I remembered you didn't have it with you when you boarded in New Orleans."

"I didn't," Keller agreed, "and I have to say I missed it."

"Well, we'll get you right on back to New Orleans, Mr. Edwards. And to that splendid hat."

࿇

A CUP OF hot chocolate in the café car, a decent night's sleep, a good breakfast. Back in his roomette, he got out the Pablo phone and placed a call.

"I'm on the train," he told Dot. "We just passed through Yazoo City."

"Has it changed much?"

"I didn't get too good a look at it. I'll be home in a few hours."

"Well, I'm glad to hear it. And glad to hear your voice, but not entirely sure why I'm hearing it. Something I should know?"

"That's a good question," he said, "and I'm hoping you can find out the answer. I wonder if anything interesting happened yesterday north and west of Chicago."

There was a pause. Then she said, "Google's not that hot on a cell phone."

"Not for an elaborate search, no."

"And the reception's a little uncertain on a moving train."

"Or even a stationary one, if it's in the middle of Mississippi."

"That where Yazoo City is? But I won't be looking for Yazoo City, will I? Tell me the name of the damn town, because I can't come up with it."

"Baker's Bluff," he said.

"Right, of course. This may take a while, Pablo. Don't go anywhere."

Where would he go? He left the phone on and stuck it in his shirt pocket and picked up the timetable, a hefty volume with schedules for all Amtrak trains. The front cover opened up to a map of all the routes, and while Keller was by no means seeing it for the first time, it never failed to engage him. He could sit there plotting out the various ways you could get from Tampa to Seattle, assuming of course that you had reason to be in Tampa, and reason to go to Seattle. The Sunset Limited ran between New Orleans and Los Angeles, and he thought he might like to ride it someday, with Julia and Jenny, although he wasn't sure how crazy Julia might be about trains. He somehow knew Jenny would like them.

There was a time, he knew, when the Sunset Limited had run all the way from Jacksonville to L.A., but some years ago they'd cut out the Jacksonville-to-New Orleans stretch. It still showed on the map as a dotted line, which indicated the service was suspended.

Keller thought this was a damned shame. Now if you wanted to go from New Orleans to Miami, say, you had to go hundreds of miles out of your way.

No, the hell with that. He didn't even want to think about it. Now a long run north and west, that looked interesting. The City of New Orleans to Chicago—he could imagine how courtly

Ainslie would be toward Jenny—and then the Empire Builder up and across, through North Dakota and Montana and clear to Seattle…

He'd dozed off, and when the phone rang it took him a moment to recognize it as such. He answered it and said hello, and Dot said, "Well, I guess I don't have to give the money back."

"What happened?"

"Jesus," she said. "What didn't?"

⁂

JULIA AND JENNY picked him up from the station. They went straight home, and after an early dinner Keller took Jenny into his stamp room for story time. He wasn't much good at making up bedtime stories, and reading her books to her bored both of them in equal measure, but she loved to sit on his lap while he turned the pages of one of his albums and told her about the stamps and where they were from.

His collection, worldwide stamps from 1840 to 1940, was housed in sixteen binders, their contents in alphabetical order. This evening Jenny pointed to an album in the middle of the second shelf and he opened it at random and told her a little about Memel, which was the German name for the city the Lithuanians called Klaipėda. There were around 130 different stamps issued for Memel from 1920 through 1922, all of them German and French stamps overprinted for use in the district. Then in 1923 Lithuanian forces occupied the place, and issued 15 stamps of their own, most but not all of them overprints. A year later the League of Nations approved the designation of Memel—well, better make that Klaipėda—as a semi-autonomous district of Lithuania.

Keller had the country complete, including most but not all of the errors listed in his Scott catalogue—here an inverted overprint, there a double surcharge. All were inexpensive, except for one set of four surcharged Klaipėda stamps worth just over a thousand dollars; Keller's set had been certified as genuine by an expert, but he had his doubts. And none of them were what you could call visually appealing, or of any conceivable interest to anyone other than a fairly devout philatelist.

And yet Jenny gave every indication of being fascinated by what he told her. She repeated the country's two names, Memel and Klaipėda, with such precision that Keller found himself wondering if he was pronouncing them correctly himself. It would be a hell of a thing, he thought, for her to be the only kid her age in Louisiana who'd ever heard of the place, and then for her to be saying it wrong.

He said as much to Julia, after Jenny was bedded down for the night. "For me," he said, "it's about as good as it gets, sitting with her and pointing at stamps and telling her stuff. And she seems to enjoy it, but I'm damned if I can figure out why."

"You're kidding, right?"

"Not at all. She gets to hear a lot of blather about stuff that happened ages before anybody she knows was born, in places nobody ever heard of. Sometimes there'll be animals on the stamps, or scenery, but most of the stamps have nothing to look at but the occasional dead king."

"You show her where the countries are," she said. "On the globe."

"Well, sure."

"And she gets to cuddle up on her daddy's lap, and be talked to like a grown-up. And she gets to learn things, which as you may have noticed is very important to her."

"Yes, it seems to be."

"She gets that from her mother. So tell me what happened in Baker's Bluff."

◦

HE TOLD HER about the Wet Spot and the Spotted Tiger, and how he'd blown the whole mission trying to find out what rhymed with El Paso.

"Once we were all three at that table together," he said, "drinking our beer straight out of the bottle, well, it was time for me to pack up and come home. What makes my job possible, what allows me to do what I do and not be looking over my shoulder all the time, is that there's no connection between me and the, uh—"

"Dead guy on the floor."

"Uh, right. Nobody can put me with the client or the dead guy, so nobody looks at me twice. But if I'm seen hanging out in public with someone—"

"I understand."

"But then I got to thinking," he said. And he told her about the rest of the conversation in the Spotted Tiger.

"You set up a threesome for them."

"I may have nudged the conversation in that direction."

"Why? Because it was a way to do something kinky but from a distance?"

"No."

"Not that there's anything wrong with that," she said. "But it doesn't sound like you."

"Dot hates to give money back," he said.

"Well, there's a surprise. I mean, doesn't everybody?"

"It bothers her more than most people. But she said fine, come home, I'll send the money back and get us out of it. And I thought maybe there's a way to keep the money."

"What if she just forgets to send a refund? It's not like he can take her to court."

He shook his head. "Word gets around," he said. "It's bad policy, and simpler to give it back. And here I was, knowing exactly what time Cowboy Roy and Pistol Pete were going to be two points on a triangle on Robin's Nest Drive."

The penny dropped. "You made a phone call."

"Isn't there something about if you show a gun in Act One it has to get fired before the final curtain comes down?"

"Chekhov, but what was the gun?"

"My third phone, the burner. Purchased for the sole purpose of calling the client if I had to, and there was never a time when I had to."

"But you still had the phone."

"Right."

"And knew what number to call. What did you tell him? Hurry home and you can watch your wife make the beast with three backs?"

"That she'd be expecting not one but two gentleman guests, and that what she didn't know was that they had an agenda. That once they'd tired of having sex with her, their plan was to kill her and rob the house."

"And he believed all of this, of course."

"If it had been the first of April," he said, "he might have suspected something. But why wouldn't he buy the whole package? I helped him see how it was his chance to be a hero. Get there right around four, walk in with a gun, and do what needs to be done. He'd be saving her life, he'd be a romantic figure in her eyes, and—"

"And they'd live happily ever after. You can almost hear the movie soundtrack, can't you?"

"Just about."

"Did he know who was calling him?"

"I said I was somebody who didn't know him at all, just a well-meaning stranger who wanted to do the right thing."

"Well, all of that was true enough."

"When he pressed a little, I let on that I was a friend of one of the pair, that I'd done time with him in Joliet."

"Oh, were they criminals?"

"Not that I know of, but I figured the more I made them sound like desperate characters, the less likely he'd be to show up without a gun."

She nodded, thinking about it. "And then you ended the call and went to Chicago and—"

"No, I was already in Chicago. I called him from Chicago."

"And that was that. There was nothing more for you to do. It would play out one way or the other, and Dot would keep the money or give it back, and either way you washed your hands of it."

"Literally," he said. "Because I ditched the burner in the men's room, and on my way out I washed my hands."

"And I guess Dot doesn't have to give the money back."

"No."

"What happened?"

"Dot gave me a pretty sketchy summary," he said, "but we can probably watch it in a month or two."

"We can watch it?"

"On *Dateline*."

"They had their party, and the husband crashed it."

"I don't know what time Roy and Pete showed up, but it wouldn't have been much after 3:15, as eager as they were. Four o'clock's what I told Todd, and it wouldn't have mattered if he was fifteen minutes early or fifteen minutes late. I guess he walked right in, and I guess they were too busy doing things to listen for doors opening and closing."

"Doing things."

"Well. Hard to know exactly what happened, who said what and who did what, but he must have walked in with a gun in his hand and he couldn't have waited too long before he started using it."

"And Roy had a gun, didn't he?"

"In the Spotted Tiger, unless he was just patting himself on the butt. No, I think the report Dot found mentioned an exchange of gunfire, so maybe Roy or Pete had time to get a couple of shots off."

"So to speak. Oh."

"Oh?"

"They're all dead, aren't they?"

He nodded.

"If there was a survivor," she said, "it wouldn't be so hard to know the sequence of events."

"Overmont survived long enough to call 911. Even if he caught a bullet along the way, it couldn't have been enough to stop him from getting the call through."

"What did he say?"

"Gave his name and address, said he'd just killed two men who were raping his wife. And then there was another gunshot, and nothing after that."

"He shot himself."

"Or maybe what they heard on the 911 call was him shooting Melania, and then he rang off and decided he didn't really want to hang around and wait for the cops to get there. By the time they did, he'd stuck a gun in his mouth and cheated some defense attorney out of a good fee."

"And the cops walked in on a bedroom full of dead people. Naked dead people, I suppose."

"Except for Overmont."

She was silent for a moment, then raised her hand to her face to cover a yawn. "I'm tired," she said, "and you must be exhausted. I know you slept on the train, but it's not the same, is it?"

AND A LITTLE later, in their bed, she stretched like a cat. "Oh, I feel much better now," she said. "I really missed you. I'm glad you're back."

"Me too."

"When they asked you if you'd ever done—what did they call it, a tag team? And you said you hadn't."

"Right."

"Was that true? Or did you ever hook up with two girls?"

"Never did either."

"Neither did I. What sheltered lives we've both led. I don't think I would want to."

"No."

"And yet it's appealing on a pure fantasy level. Isn't that strange? Why should it be exciting to imagine something that you really wouldn't want to do in a million years? Do you know what I mean?"

"I do."

"In fact, just a few minutes ago, when we were…"

"Enjoying each other's company."

"Uh-huh. I was imagining having another person in the bed with us."

"It doesn't seem to have inhibited you."

"No, it was hot, wasn't it? Maybe sometime we could, you know, bring the fantasy to bed with us."

"Not another person, but the fantasy of another person."

"Uh-huh. Talking about it, playing with the idea. That might be fun."

"It might."

"You know, I sometimes truly don't know what to make of myself. I'm a dutiful faithful wife and a loving mother, a model of middle-class morality, and I can fantasize about three-way sex while four people are spread out on white tables in the morgue in Bailey's Bluff, Illinois."

"Baker's Bluff. And I don't know if the town's big enough to have its own morgue."

"That's something else we could Google, but probably won't. Though we'll most likely find out when it's on *Dateline*. Do you really think it'll be on *Dateline?*"

"Unless *48 Hours* gets there first."

"Won't it be hard to get an hour out of it? I mean all they've got is the 911 call and the crime scene. Though I guess there'll be interviews with neighbors, his colleagues from work, anybody who knew her. Melania?"

"That's right."

"Todd and Melania Overmont. Well, those are good *Dateline* names, aren't they? Will they tie in the Marlboro Man?"

"Harold? I'm sure they will. My guess is they'll figure Roy or Pete killed him in order to get a clear shot at her."

"That hammer you bought—"

"Well, if they found Pete and Roy dead, and one had his head bashed in and the other had a hammer in his hand—"

"That's what was going to happen?"

He nodded. "Until the Late Great Marty Robbins ruined it for me."

"I always loved that song. Oh, you know what I bet happened? Todd shot both the men, Roy and Pete, and Roy tried to get his gun off the bedside table, and maybe he got off a shot and maybe he didn't, but he wound up dead and so did Pete."

"Well, I think we know that much is true."

"No there's more. And then Melania wrapped her arms around Roy, or it could have been Pete—"

"Roy's more likely."

"And she's all, 'Oh, how could you do this?' when Todd was hoping for something more along the lines of 'My Hero!' And he finally sees her for what she really is, and he empties the gun into her."

"And then reloads? Because he'd need one more bullet."

"Roy's gun. He picks up Roy's gun, calls 911, and then finishes the job. I was wondering how *Dateline* was going to get an hour out of it, and now I'm beginning to think it'll be one of their two-hour episodes. The less they know for sure, the more room they'll have for speculation. Do you suppose they'll interview the kid from the supermarket?"

"If they find him."

"'She was a nice lady. It was always a pleasure to give her a hand.' How long do you think it'll be before it airs?"

"No idea."

"I can't wait," she said. "Oh."

"What?"

"Well, you're not going to chase the story on the internet, so will you watch it on *Dateline?*"

He nodded. "That's different," he said. "That's television."

"We'll have a little premiere in front of the TV set. I won't run out and buy a new outfit for the occasion, but I'll dress up nice." She squeezed his hand. "And you can wear your fedora."